Fair Play?

"Justine," Danny said, "I can't handle playing on the same team as you."

I did my best to stare at him coldly. "Are you saying that you want me to quit?"

I could see the relief flood over Danny's face. "It's the only way, Jus. This isn't fair—you're putting me off my game."

"And what about *my* game?"

He looked at me with pained eyes. "There's a girls' team you could play on, where you belong. Why don't you just quit and let things get back to where they were, Justine?"

I couldn't believe he was saying these things. I didn't know what to do.

"I don't think our relationship can take this stress," Danny continued. "If you keep playing here, then it's all over between us."

No More Boys

SPECIAL EDITION

No More Boys

Janet Quin-Harkin

Rainbow Bridge®
Troll Associates

Chapter 1

"Springtime at Sagebrush was never like this!" I commented to my friends as I turned up the collar on my fake fur-trimmed jacket and gazed out the window at the rain-swept yard. "It never rained there."

"I thought it was in Arizona, not Camelot, Justine," Ginger said, grinning at Roni.

"It was better than Camelot," I said, tossing back my hair. "I wish I were there now."

So far, today hadn't ranked as the most fun day of my life. I had gotten drenched on the way to school, completely ruining a pair of expensive suede clogs. So I was in a bad mood even before I sat in the green Jell-O. Now I was in a definitely ugly mood. Things like green Jell-O and a cafeteria that resembled a food riot in a prison made me long for my old school again.

Last year I'd been at an exclusive boarding school in the mountains called Sagebrush Academy. My father had taken me out at the end of eighth grade so that I could attend a public high school and live at home. Talk about culture shock! Alta Mesa had over three thousand kids, most of whom had never grasped the concept of coordinating the colors of their clothes.

In fact, if I hadn't made three such terrific friends as Ginger, Roni, and Karen on the first day, I don't think I'd have survived a week. We'd become really close when we formed a Boyfriend Club to try to meet people at our big new high school. We no longer needed the club, since we had all found cute boyfriends (mine is Danny, but more about him later), but we still hung out together all the time. My friends had stuck by me when I know I must have been a snobby pain in the you-know-what. And now that I'd been here almost six months, I was actually glad I'd switched. I was enjoying every minute of high school . . . except for days like today.

"There is nothing to do on rainy lunch hours," I complained, looking up and down the dreary hallway.

"We could go see the nerds at the Computer Club," Karen said. I shot her a horrified glance.

"Puh-lease! I'd rather be boiled in oil," I said. Then I saw that she'd been kidding. Karen is good at making people take her seriously—especially me. I grinned at her.

We had been drifting up and down the hallways, while the wind and rain battered the windows, making the whole building groan and shudder. We didn't have much of a winter in Phoenix, but when we did, it was fierce. The storm had gone on for two days now and had prevented us from eating lunch under our favorite tree. And two days in the cafeteria with three zillion noisy, immature, badly dressed kids was enough to make any sane person lose their cool.

"I don't think I can take another lunch in the cafeteria. It's too stressful," I said.

"No kidding," Roni sighed. "I know I ate too quickly just to get out of that place. Now I feel sick."

"Me, too," Karen agreed. "The noise level in that cafeteria has given me the world's worst headache. Why does everyone have to yell? And why did they build it with a ceiling that echoes?"

"And why do they let in so many dumb boys?" Ginger added. "I really resent getting hit in the head with a flying tortilla."

"At least you didn't sit in the green Jell-O," I told her. "Now I'll have to throw out a perfectly good skirt."

"Justine!" Ginger cried. She looked horrified. "Jell-O will wash out, you know. Just give it a pre-soak first and scrub it with a little bleach."

It was my turn to look horrified. "Me? Scrub? I can open a washing machine and throw in some detergent, but that's it. If the stains don't come out, then too bad. Goodbye skirt."

They all laughed. Ever since I had met Roni, Ginger, and Karen, I had kept them amused. Not intentionally, of course. Most of the time I didn't even realize I'd said something funny. They thought I was acting like a snob when I said I'd throw out a skirt with a stain on it, but my stepmother would do the same thing. Everyone I had known at Sagebrush would have, too.

"I just don't *do* scrubbing," I told my friends. "One of you can have the skirt if it will fit you."

Roni made a face. "You know I'm not a size three, Justine. Your skirt wouldn't even go over my hips!"

"It would fit Karen," Ginger said, glancing across at her.

Karen shook her head furiously. "Much as I would love to have one of Justine's skirts, you know my parents would both have cardiac arrest if I went out in a miniskirt and dared to let people see my knees." Karen has the world's strictest parents.

"You're going to have to educate them someday, Karen," Ginger said.

"I am, but slowly. I now have two pairs of jeans, which is a miracle. I don't wear plaid anymore. I've been out with makeup on and they haven't even noticed. We're getting there."

"At the rate you're moving, you'll be into your first pair of shorts when you graduate from college," Roni said.

Karen laughed. "Are you kidding? Once I get away to college, I'll wear what I want. I'm going to go crazy and wear every freaky thing I can think of. I'll be Karen the funky dresser!"

"Then you and James really will look like a couple," Ginger chuckled, "if you're still together by then." James was Karen's boyfriend, and he was known for his bizarre taste in clothes, like long flowing black capes and red suspenders. Personally I would rather die than go out with a guy who looked like that, but Karen didn't seem to notice. She just looked all embarrassed as she always did when James was discussed.

"Who knows?" she said. "Maybe we'll go to the same college."

"True love at Harvard?" Ginger quipped. Karen was also really smart. She probably *would* go to Harvard.

I don't even like to think about tomorrow, let alone college four years away. Maybe that's because I've never stayed in one place long enough to feel secure. My dad was always moving me around until he married my stepmother. Now they're trying to make us into a real family, complete with a new baby on the way. That also freaked me out to start with. But I'm getting used to the idea of a baby. And I'm also getting along better with my stepmother. I like being part of a normal family.

Suddenly everything else went out of my mind as I noticed a new poster on the wall. "Hey, guys, look!" I yelled, grabbing Karen's arm. "There's going to be a Valentine's Day Dance."

We crowded around the poster. "Cool," Ginger said. "Live music, too, not that terrible DJ we had for the Homecoming Dance."

I forgot all about the ruined clogs, the stain on my skirt, the rain on the windows. "I'm so excited!" I said. I started jumping up and down and waving my arms. I know I do that when I'm excited. I can't stop myself. "That's just what we need to chase away the winter blues. I wonder how formal it is. I'll have to buy a new dress. Red or pink, do you think? Strapless or not?"

"Justine, calm down," Karen said, holding my arm firmly. "You're going to hit somebody."

"This was just the lift I needed," I said. "I love having something to look forward to. And you know I love shopping for new clothes more than anything. Let's all go to the mall on Saturday and find me the world's most gorgeous prom dress."

"Not until we find out what everyone else is wearing, Justine," Roni said. "Remember the Freshman

Welcome Dance when we were the only ones in dresses, thanks to you?"

"Gee, I hope everyone isn't wearing jeans this time," I said. "I hope it's formal. I'm dying for a new dress. My one regret about not staying with the Kestrels is that they have formals every month—I could have bought a dress for every one!"

"I think a formal function with that snobby sorority would be worse than an afternoon at the dentist," Roni commented.

"You're right," I said. "They were a bunch of jerks. I'm glad I'm not with them anymore. It's just that I love getting dressed up."

"So get Danny to take you to more formals," Ginger said.

"Danny?" I could feel the grin spread across my face. "Please! He's not exactly Mr. Formality. He's only happy when he's wearing that disgusting old plaid shirt and dirty jeans."

"I can't believe you haven't managed to make him wear designer flannel shirts yet, Justine," Karen said with a grin.

"Are you kidding? Danny's the most strong-minded person I've ever met," I said. "You can't get him to do anything he doesn't want to do. Actually, I think that's why we're still together. He doesn't let me walk all over him."

"I can't believe that you've stayed with him for so long," Roni commented. "I thought it was doomed from the start. I mean, the princess and the garbage man—it sounds like a movie!"

"For your information," I said frostily, "I am not a princess and Danny's dad happens to own the biggest garbage company in town. And I don't care if we have nothing in common because he makes me laugh. I like that. And he hates phonies. I like that, too."

Ginger nudged Karen. "She didn't mention that he also has great muscles and cute brown eyes."

I smiled. "I especially like that. He looks great in a tux. I really hope this dance is formal."

"I just hope I'm going," Karen said. "You know what James thinks about organized school functions."

"You have to come, Karen," I said, shaking her arm. "It won't be fun unless we're all there."

"Ben doesn't like dances either," Ginger said. "He worries about making a fool of himself on the dance floor. But I'm sure we'll go if he knows I really want to. After all, Valentine's Day is the most romantic day of the year. I wonder if he'll send me roses . . . or maybe heart-shaped chocolates?"

Karen and I looked at each other and made gagging noises.

"Shut up, you guys," Ginger said, turning red. "I can

14

just see your faces if James and Danny send you flowers."

"James is romantic," Karen said, "but he doesn't like commercialism. He thinks that Valentine's Day is a holiday designed to make the greeting card manufacturers rich. If I get a card, it will probably be something he made on his computer."

"Well, Danny better send me a very expensive card," I said. "Maybe I should take him to the card store and point out the one I want. Otherwise I'll get one with kissing frogs or something. You know what his sense of humor is like."

"I thought you loved his sense of humor," Ginger said.

"Usually I do, but this is supposed to be romantic, right?"

They didn't get to answer because a big noisy group of kids came past us, taking up most of the hall and making us flatten ourselves against the wall as they went by. I wasn't entirely surprised to see Drew Howard in the middle of the group, talking louder than anybody. Drew was the most popular guy in the sophomore class, and he was also Roni's ex-boyfriend. I noticed that he had his arm around a perky blonde with lots of spiral curls. After they'd gone, I glanced at Roni. She looked confused.

"He didn't even say hi," she said quietly.

"Maybe he feels strange talking to you now," I

suggested. "And what's-her-face was right there with him."

"Cammy," Roni said bitterly. "Her name is Cammy. Short for Camilla." She made a face.

"Are you going to ask Chris to the dance?" Ginger asked her. Chris was Roni's current guy—not really her boyfriend, but more like a friend-friend.

"I don't know if I should ask him," Roni said, still staring down the hallway after Drew. "I can't help thinking how wonderful things would be if I were still going with Drew. A Valentine's Dance would have been just the kind of thing he loved. I guess I still miss him."

"It was your choice, remember?" Ginger said. "He begged you to take him back and you wouldn't."

"I know," Roni said with a big, dramatic sigh. "I know we're not really right for each other, but I can't help missing him. He was my first real crush, and it hurts to see him with other girls. I know he'll be at the dance with Cammy, and it will break my heart."

"Well, then, don't go to the dance," I said.

Roni looked at me as if I were crazy. "Don't go to one of the greatest events of the school year? Are you out of your mind? I wouldn't miss it for the world."

"Even if you have to dance with Chris?" I asked. "Remember, he used to hang around with the nerd pack."

"Chris is not a nerd. He's very sweet," Roni said.

Then she frowned. "I mean, he's not *really* a nerd. What do you guys think?"

"Why not go?" Karen asked. "You enjoy being with him."

"Yeah, but I've never seen him dance," Roni said. "What if he dances like Walter?"

We all groaned. One of the worst nights of our lives had been the Freshman Welcome Dance. Somehow we'd gotten stuck with the nerds all evening. They jerked and twitched like dying octopi on the dance floor. Just the thought of it embarrassed me. And Roni's friend Chris had started out as one of the nerd pack. She'd brought him into mainstream life since then, but he still had a few nerdy traits. Like getting excited about PBS documentaries on heart disease or the mating habits of the black widow spider. And he still wore those polyester pants. Danny was a champion dresser compared to Chris.

But Roni liked him. "Well . . . just do the slow dances," I said. "You can keep your head on his shoulder so he can't jump around. You wouldn't mind that, would you?"

"Not at all," Roni said. "His shoulder just happens to be the perfect height for me."

"Great, so bring him," I said. "You guys *have* to come—all of you. I'm sure Danny will be dying to go. You know him—Mr. School Spirit. Did I tell you he's going to run for sophomore class president next year?"

"Yes, Justine, about a billion times already," Ginger said.

"I guess Justine can't wait to be sophomore first lady," Karen said.

"Do you think we'll still be together by then?" I asked. "Wow, that's a long time to be with one boy."

"Nothing's wrong between you, is it?" Roni asked.

"No, everything's great."

"Then I hope you stay with Danny forever," Roni said. "He's certainly whipping you into shape."

"What's that supposed to mean?"

"I mean you didn't freak out in the cafeteria when you sat in the green Jell-O. You didn't scream the whole building down and threaten to sue, which you would have done a few months ago. And you don't tell us every two minutes about your last trip to Paris or how you took fencing at Sagebrush. You're turning into a normal person."

"Gee, thanks a lot," I said, my cheeks coloring. I knew Roni didn't mean to hurt me, but she had. I also knew that I *had* been that snobby, impossible person who would have screamed the place down if I'd sat in Jell-O. Roni was right. Danny had taught me to be able to laugh at myself. He'd also taught me how nice it felt to have someone think you were special.

Karen must have noticed that I looked upset. She's very sensitive about other people's feelings. "Isn't

Danny's last basketball game tonight, Justine?" she asked.

I nodded. "It doesn't look as if they're going to make the playoffs, so the season's over."

"Their team wasn't very good, was it?" Ginger said. "Don't get me wrong. Danny and a couple of the others were great, but there didn't seem to be much talent apart from them."

"Danny says that there aren't many jocks in the freshman class. And the ones who are jocks aren't very tall. They'd better grow before we're seniors. I hate cheering for losing teams."

"You know what I've been thinking," Ginger said slowly. "I've been thinking it's about time the guys cheered for us."

"What do you mean?" Karen asked.

"What has been our main recreational activity so far this year?" Ginger demanded. "We watch Ben and Drew and Danny play sports. Karen watches James do computer stuff. Is this all we want out of life?"

"You think it's about time we did stuff of our own?" Roni asked. "I totally agree. But I did the talent show with Chris, and I've already agreed to be in the spring play. And you saved Spirit Rock, Ginger, with the Ecology Club."

"And Karen has her violin," I added. "She knows what it feels like to be a star."

"Oh, come on," Karen said, blushing furiously. "You know I only take violin lessons because of my parents. If it were up to me, I'd rather play volleyball."

"You won't be able to play volleyball at Carnegie Hall," Roni said. "At least you've got something to aim for. I think Ginger's right about having our own sports, and not only because the guys should see that *our* lives are important, too. I'm starting to think about college. My parents won't be able to handle the tuition if I don't get some sort of scholarship."

"You have to be pretty good to get a sports scholarship," I said.

"The problem is that Oak Creek Junior High was totally chauvinistic," Ginger said. "It was boys' football and boys' basketball and boys' baseball. The only thing girls were allowed to do was be cheerleaders."

"That's true," agreed Roni. "We never got a chance to find out what sports we might be good at."

"And PE isn't exactly helping much," Karen commented. "Aerobics and body conditioning and ethnic dancing so far? I can't see us getting a scholarship in any of those fields."

"We could go look at the sports board," Ginger said. "Spring tryouts are coming up."

We headed down the hallway until we came to the glass-fronted cases containing trophies and pictures of past

Alta Mesa stars. The notice board beside them was full of stuff, but a big black-lettered flyer caught my eye first.

"Track team tryouts are this Friday," I said. "You don't need any special skills for that. Everyone knows how to run."

"You're right," Ginger said, "and I'm pretty fast. I can always beat my brother in a race."

"I keep going pretty well," Roni commented. "When I missed the bus to school, I used to take a shortcut across the fields—remember, Ginger? That must have been a couple of miles, right?"

Ginger grinned. "Maybe one-tenth of a mile."

"Well, it was uphill, both ways," Roni said with a grin.

"And you were barefoot and it was snowing," Karen finished for her. We looked at each other and smiled.

"So are we going to try out?" Ginger insisted.

"I think we should do it," I said. "I know all those years of ballet and fencing have given me grace and agility. I can just see myself hurling the javelin or pole vaulting—flying gracefully through the air like—"

I flung out my arms and hit a large guy full in the chest.

"Hey, watch it!" he growled.

"Sorry. Just practicing my pole vaulting," I said, feeling very stupid.

"What were you saying about all that grace and agility?" Roni teased.

"Never mind that," I said. "I have a big problem!"

"What?" the other three demanded.

"This only gives me three days to find the perfect outfit for tryouts. Where do you buy track outfits? Lycra bodysuit, I think, with just a touch of glitter maybe?"

"Justine, you're too much," Karen said, laughing. "They won't let you onto the team because of your clothes!"

"Don't laugh," I said. "It's true. If you look great, people think you are great. That's my philosophy. And that's why I *always* look great."

"Hey, Justine, you've got a big green blob on the back of your skirt!" a voice chirped behind me. I looked up to see Owen, head nerd, grinning at the head of the nerd pack.

"What a pity. Your nice white skirt is ruined forever," Ronald added.

"Maybe not," Owen said. "Maybe the Jell-O in the cafeteria is water soluble after all. I know we've long suspected that it had a petroleum base, but we could be wrong. Let's see." Before I could stop him, he had whipped out a disgusting handkerchief and held it under the nearest drinking fountain. Then he advanced on me. "Here, Justine, let us wipe it off for you."

"Touch me and die," I said firmly.

"We were only trying to help," Ronald said, looking hurt.

"Thanks, but we were just on our way to the girls' room to help her wipe it off," Roni said hastily, grabbing my arm before I did anything too drastic. I had a phobia about nerds. If one of them had actually touched my skirt . . . gross! I don't think I could have controlled myself. There would have been squished nerd all over the hallway.

"You see?" I muttered to my friends as they swept me down the hall. "I look yucky, I attract nerds!"

"How interesting," I heard Owen's high-pitched voice. "That stain on her skirt is in the shape of Alaska."

"I thought it looked more like a carbon molecule," Ronald commented.

"Now do you understand why I need some serious shopping before tryouts on Friday?" I asked as we went into the bathroom.

My friends grinned as they grabbed paper towels and attempted to get rid of Alaska and/or the carbon molecule on my rear end. I knew they probably thought I was being a rich, snobby princess again, but they just didn't understand. I'd never been on a track team in my life. I had a sneaking suspicion that I wouldn't be too great at it. We'd had Field Day at

Sagebrush, and I'd never won a single cup. Okay, I admit it, I came in dead last in the hundred-yard dash. So you can see why the right outfit was important to me. If I could psych out half the freshman girls by looking like Flo Jo, I might just have a chance!

Chapter

2

For the next few days we tried to put the Valentine's Dance out of our minds, while we concentrated on track tryouts. We used our lunch hours to try to whip ourselves into shape by jogging around the football field and doing sit-ups. A little late, maybe, but better than nothing. I was worrying more about the most important aspect of track—my outfit.

By the time tryouts came along on Friday, I'd found it. It wasn't designed for running, but it looked great on me and it felt great, too. It was really a tennis outfit— pink knit shorts, a striped pink-and-white top, and even a matching hooded pink sweatshirt, for workouts on cold days. This was really good, because my favorite Reeboks had pink trim. All I needed to make the outfit complete was pink socks and a pink scrunchie. No one could say now that Justine Craft didn't dress to kill!

I produced the outfit in the locker room after school. "How about this?" I demanded. "Cute or what?"

"Wow," Roni said, looking at it admiringly. "Really cute."

She was in the middle of putting on her regular PE shorts. So was Karen. Ginger was wearing an old Oak Creek Panthers T-shirt. None of them had taken any trouble about their appearance at all, which was a shame. I mean, if I were a coach and I were picking a team, I'd want people who looked like they were a credit to the school.

"And it's comfortable too," I said. "I can really move well in it."

"Too bad you couldn't find one with glitter on it," Ginger said. "Did you try calling Jackie Joyner-Kersee for the name of her designer?"

For a second I thought she was serious, but then I saw her wink at Karen. I blushed. *They're just jealous,* I told myself. *Well, I'll show them. Wait until I'm the star of the team. . . .* I closed my eyes as I swept my hair up into the pink scrunchie, seeing the headlines in the school newspaper: "Freshman Track Star Takes State Title. An Olympic Berth for Budding Phoenix star?"

"Are you ready yet, Justine?" Karen yelled. "Everyone else is already out there. Come on, we're going without you."

I gave my hair a quick mist of super-hold spray gel and ran out to join them. In fact, I jogged all the way over to the coach. Let him see that I moved with the grace of a young gazelle and had energy to spare!

"All right, ladies," he said, looking around at us as if we were the worst bunch of athletes he'd ever seen. "I'm Coach Parker. I've been coaching track for twenty years, and I've produced quite a few champions in my time. Today you'll all run a sprint. You'll all run a half mile. And you'll all rotate among the field events. I've got a couple of varsity team members watching each station for me, and after we've taken stats, I'll tell you where I can use you."

His gaze had been moving steadily around the circle and now it came to me. I saw his eyes shoot open wide, blink, then move on again. *He's impressed,* I thought. *Nobody else took the trouble to come out looking their best.*

I looked around at the other girls. Some of them were staring at me. Were they really freshmen? They looked awfully big and mean.

"Okay, listen up," Coach Parker growled. "First we do fifteen minutes of warm-ups, then I'll divide you into groups. Let's get moving."

By the end of the warm-ups, I was pretty tired. So was Karen. "I hope we don't get the half mile first," she whispered to me.

27

"I hope we don't get the half mile at all. I don't think I could stagger that far," I whispered back. Tough, muscular girls were jogging around me, looking like frisky race horses, as if they couldn't wait to get started. I shot Karen a despairing look. "Do we really want to be on a track team, anyway?" I said. "Do we really want our afternoons all tied up like this?"

"Quit talking and start running," the coach barked. "You girls over there . . . yes, you in the pink . . . whatever . . . do the hundred-yard dash."

We dashed. I wasn't quite last, but I wasn't near the front either. Ginger was. She came in third, and the girl taking the times asked for her name.

We tried long jumping, but when I found that you had to land on your butt in wet sand, I said no thank you to that one. I didn't want a horrible mud stain on the back of my new white shorts! I'd had enough of stains to last me for a while. I felt the same about the high jump, too. In addition to that, it looked pretty impossible.

"Some of you might not have been taught how to high jump," the coach said. "That's okay. Do your best. Get over the bar whatever way suits you today. Donna here is my star high jumper. She'll show you what you're aiming for."

Donna, almost six feet tall and all legs, trotted over and placed the bar higher than most people's heads.

Then she jogged up to the bar and flung herself over it backward. Her head went over and the rest of her followed. Totally amazing!

"Hey, that was neat," Karen said, watching her. She went up to the girl. "Could you do that once more, please? I'm interested to see how you get your hips that high."

"It's simple really," the girl said. "Your head's the heaviest part of you. If you can get your head over, the rest will follow. It's all in the mind. You just have to visualize it."

"Yeah, right!" I muttered. But Karen was still staring as if she was mesmerized. When the coach asked who wanted to try, Karen raised her hand. She jogged up to the bar, which was now a foot lower, and she went over, just like Donna had done. Roni and I stared in amazement as Karen came running back to us, looking excited and happy. "It was just like she said," she exclaimed. "I pictured it in my head and I just did it. Hey, that was fun. I want to try again."

The girl came over and wrote down Karen's name before we went on to the next event. I could tell before we started that the half mile was not going to be my thing. Well, maybe I wasn't fast, but I was sure I was the only one who had taken years of ballet. I decided to concentrate on being graceful. I started out pretending I was crossing a ballet stage, with pointed toes and elegantly swinging arms.

29

I was behind by the first turn. I was last by the first time around the track. I was way last by the time we came in. And I wasn't very pleased to see that Roni was being asked her name for finishing among the leaders. Now all my friends had been able to shine in one event, except for me.

"Excuse me," I said to the coach. "I was wondering when we get to try pole vaulting. I've had ballet and gymnastics training, so I'm sure I'd be good at that."

I heard giggles coming from behind me. "Little lady, gals don't pole vault," he said. "That's just a guys' event."

"But that's so sexist," I said.

I saw him frown. "That's because most girls don't have the upper-body strength to push themselves into a handstand in midair," he said. "If you can do a couple hundred push-ups, I'll think about giving you a shot at it." Then he grinned and walked away.

What a chauvinist. "I hate him," I muttered to Karen. "Did you hear how he spoke to me? He called me little lady!"

Karen gave me a sympathetic shrug. "I guess he's just like that," she said.

"Well, I don't even think I want to be part of a team with him as a coach," I said loudly.

"Oh, but Justine, we're all going to be doing it,"

Karen said. "It wouldn't be fun if you weren't there with us. Please give it another try."

It's hard to say no to Karen because she's so nice.

"I'm sorry," I muttered, "but I can't see anything that I'd be good at."

I didn't look at anyone as I walked back to the locker room. I was still sitting there, in my new pink-and-white outfit, when my friends came back, talking excitedly.

"Justine?" Roni said. "What happened?"

"I decided that track wasn't for me," I said.

"But Justine, it's going to be such fun," Karen began.

I shook my head. "Maybe for you. You can do things. But not me. You saw me out there. I was terrible. I couldn't do a thing."

"But we'll all be training after school and going to meets on weekends," Ginger said. "It won't be the same if you're not there."

"It's okay, I'll survive," I said, even though I wasn't completely sure I would. What would I do after school if I had no friends to gossip with on the phone?

And there was something else. I hated the thought that they were all better than me, even Karen, whom I had never thought of as a potential jock. I'd always thought I was the athletic one. I was used to being the one who could do things, who had been all over the

31

world. Now I was Justine, the failure. I didn't know if I could handle that.

"I don't understand it," I said. "I just don't understand why I can't run fast. I move pretty darned quickly when I'm on a tennis court."

"Then why don't you try out for the tennis team?" Ginger said.

I stared at her. "Tennis team? Are you saying there are tryouts for a tennis team?"

Ginger looked surprised. "Sure. Didn't you see the notice?"

I grabbed her shoulders, shaking her like a rag doll. "Notice? What notice? Where?"

"When we were mooching through the halls that day. There was a little notice up at the corner of the sports board. I thought you'd seen it."

"We had to run when the nerds showed up, remember?" I said.

She nodded. "It was only a small typed notice, not a great big thing like the track tryouts."

"Obviously designed for superior people who can read small letters," I said. Ginger rolled her eyes, but my self-confidence was returning rapidly. Who needed a crummy track team when there were tennis tryouts? "Most tennis players are intelligent, sophisticated people," I went on. "Did I ever tell you I went to the same tennis camp as Andre Agassi?"

I saw my friends' raised eyebrows and shut up quickly.

"I say go for it, Justine," Karen said. "You're always talking about how good you are at tennis. You might be the star of the team."

"I really might," I said happily. Then I noticed the way they were looking at me. "Look, you guys, I know I tend to talk big sometimes. I know I've bragged about things I did at Sagebrush and they weren't always true. But tennis really is something I can do. I really have been to some top-class camps. I really was one of the best players at Sagebrush. Maybe I *will* be the star!"

As I said it a picture came into my head: myself in a new white tennis outfit standing in the middle of the court, holding a big silver cup over my head while everyone cheered. At last I was going to be the sort of person I'd dreamed of being. At last I was going to make my mark at Alta Mesa.

"Oh, no," I exclaimed, suddenly coming down to earth.

"What? Can't you make tryouts tomorrow?"

"Sure, but I have almost no time at all to buy a new tennis outfit!"

"Justine!" Roni exclaimed. "What's wrong with the one you're wearing?"

"But I bought that for track," I said.

They all started laughing.

"You guys don't understand," I snapped. "In my mind now this outfit is associated with my failure as a track star. I need a new outfit to boost my confidence."

"Justine, you really are something else," Ginger said, giving Roni a quick glance. "If you're good enough for the tennis team, you'll make it. It doesn't matter if you're wearing old sweats or your bathrobe."

"Dummy, I couldn't serve in a bathrobe," I said, making them laugh even harder. I looked from one face to the next. They were all happy about having made the track team. They didn't see that I was really scared. I didn't want to be the only person to feel like a total failure. For once in my life, I wanted to feel like a star!

Chapter

3

After track tryouts, I wanted to go shopping for a new tennis outfit, but I made the mistake of asking my stepmother to drive me to the mall. She asked me why, and I told her I had to have a new outfit for tennis tryouts. Well, she hit the roof. You'd have thought I'd asked her for a new BMW convertible, instead of an itsy-bitsy tennis skirt. She seemed to think that the outfit I'd bought for track tryouts was just fine—which shows how clueless parents can be. Just when I was starting to like her better, too. She was totally acting like the wicked witch again. Just because she was tired all the time now that she was pregnant.

So I wasn't in the best of moods when I met my friends outside the gym that night. We'd been going to cheer for Danny's basketball games all season. At least,

I'd been going to all his games, and I started dragging my friends along because I figured his team needed all the help they could get. Besides, I felt lonely sitting in the bleachers by myself. I don't like doing anything alone.

Usually I could persuade at least one of my friends to come with me, unless they had plans with their boyfriends. Tonight I had all three. Ginger's boyfriend Ben was doing something with her brother Todd, who happens to be his best friend. Roni's friend Chris still has this touch of geekiness. He's not really into spirit things like basketball. And tonight he was doing something with his friends, the nerds. They'd never show up at a basketball game—Owen the shrimp was scared that someone would stuff him through the basketball hoop.

So I had both Ginger and Roni for moral support. Then, just as we were about to go into the gym, I saw Karen.

"I thought she was doing something with James tonight," I muttered to Roni.

Roni dug me in the ribs. "She's got James with her!"

I did a double take. "That's a first," I whispered. "James at a basketball game? By the end of the year she might have turned him into a human being, if only she could get him to dress normally!"

James was actually dressed conservatively—for him. He was not wearing his black Zorro hat or his long flowing cape. But he *was* wearing a striped T-shirt and

36

bright red suspenders, like something out of Doctor Seuss. I shuddered.

"You couldn't pay me enough to walk beside a guy dressed like that," I whispered to Roni. "Unless, of course, it was to a costume party."

Roni grinned. "Hey, Karen, over here," she yelled through the crowd.

Karen came over to us, dragging James after her so that she looked like a tug towing a large cruise ship. "Hi, guys," she called.

"Hi, James," Roni said.

"Hi." He didn't even look at us. He looked as if he were on his way to the dentist.

"We thought you two had plans for this evening," Ginger said.

Karen glanced back at James. "I sort of wanted to watch the last basketball game," she said. James said nothing. We made our way into the gym. Karen and James sat a couple of rows below us. We always like the very top. Then you can rest your back against the gym wall. I watched Karen and James whispering together. Then I saw her look away as if she were mad.

Danny's team came out and began warming up.

"Do you think they've got a shot at winning this one?" Ginger asked me. "It would be kind of nice if they finished the season with one win."

37

"No kidding," I said. "Danny gets depressed because his team's so bad. You know how competitive he is."

"But what can you do when most of the team is made up of midgets," Roni said with a hopeless smile. "Look at the Scottsdale Panthers—they've got some freshman six-footers. We've only got that guy Brent and he always drops the ball."

The Scottsdale Panthers looked pretty impressive as they started their layup drill.

"Why is that?" Ginger asked. "Do you think they put something in the water in other parts of Phoenix to make the other teams grow bigger than ours?"

"Let's just hope our guys are late bloomers. We have a good varsity, don't we? Maybe these guys will shoot up over the summer," Roni said.

The game started. It was clear in the first five minutes that our team was not going to post its only win of the season. It was pretty sad, actually, but I'd gotten used to it by now. I cheered anyway. Danny heard my voice and looked up to give me a smile as he made a great pass, only to see the ball stolen from one of his teammates.

"Poor Danny. I bet he's glad the season's over tonight," Ginger whispered.

I nodded.

"Are you guys doing anything after the game?"

"I don't know. We didn't talk about it," I said. "I guess not, because the game won't be over until late and I've got tennis tryouts tomorrow at nine." I shuddered. "Nine o'clock on a Saturday morning? How can they be so inconsiderate? Don't they realize people need to sleep in and watch cartoons?"

"It's worth it," Ginger said. "You're going to be the star tennis player."

"I'm just praying I make the team," I said. "Now that you guys are all going to be track stars, I don't want to look like a total failure."

"You're going to be fine," Ginger said firmly. "All those tennis camps have got to pay off, right?"

I just hoped they would. I tried not to think about tennis tryouts while I watched Danny. I wondered what it would be like if I made the team and really were a tennis star, and he came to cheer for me. Wouldn't that be something?

At halftime we were down by twenty-five points. Danny's head was bowed as they slunk back to the locker room. He was playing his heart out, but there just weren't enough jocks on the team. I watched James head down to the snack bar. As soon as he'd gone, Karen came flying up to join us.

"James is being such a pain," she complained.

"Why? What's wrong?"

"He didn't want to come tonight. You know what he's like about school spirit—he thinks it's ridiculous. But I wanted to see the last game. I said we always did what he wanted and it was about time we did something that I wanted. I guess he was surprised, so he said okay. But now that he's here, he keeps making all these negative comments about it being a waste of time and how he could have been trying out his new computer program."

"What's with these guys?" Ginger demanded. "Ben isn't quite as bad, but he always thinks that what he wants to do is more important than what I want to do. Tonight he and Todd decided they wanted to see this action movie, and I said I hated watching people get blown up. So they went without me! If it had been the other way around, Ben would have sulked for days."

"Chris is the same," Roni said. "He knows what I think about the nerds, yet he still does stuff with them. He's at some kind of horror movie with them right now, because he hates to say no to Owen."

"Hates to say no to Owen?" I said, wrinkling my nose in disgust. "Everybody says no to Owen."

"Exactly," she said. "He feels bad for Owen, because everybody treats him like pond scum."

"He *is* pond scum."

Roni shook her head. "He was the only one who was

40

nice to Chris when Chris first moved here," she said. "So Chris feels an obligation to be nice to him."

"Chris needs his head examined," I grumbled.

"He's just a sweet guy," Roni said. "In fact, I'm lucky . . ." Her voice trailed off. Drew had arrived. As usual, he was in the middle of a big group of kids. He had popcorn in one hand and a soda in the other, and he was heading in our direction. As the group came up the steps, Drew noticed Roni.

"Hey, babe," he called. "How's it going?"

"Pretty good, thanks. How about you?"

"Pretty good." He was almost level with us now. "Did you see the notice about the Valentine's Day Dance?"

Roni nodded. "Uh-huh."

"So are you going?"

"I haven't decided yet."

"It's going to be great. Good band. You have to come—I'm counting on it."

Drew's group had moved along the bleachers. He saw that he was being left behind and gave Roni one of his dazzling smiles. "Gotta go," he said, and hurried to catch up with them.

Roni was sitting in a trance. "Did you hear that?" she whispered. "Was that an invitation or what?"

"Why would he have brought it up if he wasn't inviting you?" I said.

"But what about what's-her-face—Cammy? Did they break up?" Ginger asked.

"I don't know," Roni said.

"Do you really want to get back together with Drew?" Karen asked. "I thought you'd decided that you two were too different."

"And what about Chris?" Ginger reminded her.

Roni made a face and ran her hand through her dark hair. "I don't know," she said. "I like Chris. But think about it, guys—Valentine's Dance with Drew? Wouldn't that be pretty special? Can you imagine . . . Drew in a tux, me in a new slinky black dress. Wow!" She grabbed Karen and me, and pulled us together. "This is a job for the Boyfriend Club," she whispered. "Find out the scoop about Drew and Cammy. I don't want to get my hopes up if she's still around."

"Okay, we'll see what we can do," I said.

"Ben will probably know. They're in the same classes," Ginger said. "I can ask him tomorrow—if he takes the time out of his busy schedule to talk to me!"

This was what the Boyfriend Club was good at— finding out the scoop on things at school for each other, asking questions that we'd be too embarrassed to ask for ourselves.

James appeared with drinks for him and Karen.

"I have to go and stop him from being such a baby,"

she said. "See you guys tomorrow. Good luck in your tryouts, Justine."

The second half started and turned into an embarrassing rout. There wasn't even anything to cheer for anymore. Danny fouled out because he was trying to stop the Scottsdale Panthers single-handedly. After that, the Panthers scored at will. It was a pretty subdued crowd that filed out of the gym. I said goodbye to my friends and went around to the locker room to wait for Danny.

"Hey," he said, his face lighting up as he saw me standing there. "Pathetic game, right?"

"You were great," I said, leaning over to give him a quick kiss on the cheek. "I don't care how the rest of the team played. You still looked good."

He grinned. "I wish," he said. "Boy, am I glad basketball is over and we can move on to something else."

"Guess what?" I said excitedly. "I'm trying out for the tennis team tomorrow."

"No kidding? That's great, Justine. And it's an amazing coincidence, because I'm going out for tennis, too."

"You are? I thought you were a baseball nut."

"I was, but I heard the tennis team is kind of weak, and the coach asked me if I'd consider playing tennis this year. And being the wonderful guy that I am . . ." He chuckled.

"Yeah, right," I said, giving him a friendly shove. "He

just knew how to flatter your oversized ego. He probably promised you you'd be the star of the tennis team, with your own dressing room and sponsorship from Reebok."

"And my own personal cheerleader?" Danny suggested, his eyes flirting with me. Then he sighed. "I just hope the team isn't too lame. The only real jocks in our grade are all going out for baseball."

"I hope my team isn't too *good*," I said. "I really want to make it."

He took my hand and we started to walk across the school yard to where our fathers were parked to take us home. It was still cold and windy, and it felt strange to shiver. Shivering is something we don't do often in Phoenix.

"Alta Mesa isn't known for being a big tennis school," he said, putting his jacket around my shoulders. "All the tennis stars get scholarships to Sandhurst—you know, that snobby private school? Sahndhurst, Dahling. Where do I park my Beemer?" He did the accent perfectly, along with the gestures.

"Oh, right," I said. "I know it. My dad thought about sending me there once."

He looked at me and grinned, but he didn't say anything mean. He knows I don't like being teased. "They really go in for tennis in a big way," Danny said. "They recruit like crazy. All the ranked junior players go there, and they always win the state championship."

"I'd just like to get the chance to play," I said.

"Are you a good player?" he asked.

"Not bad," I said modestly, remembering all Roni and Karen's lectures on not bragging. "I can hit the ball over the net."

"That sounds about my level," he said. "I've never had any formal training, but I've hit the ball around with my old man enough. And of course I *am* a fine natural athlete, right?"

"Yeah, and you're really modest, too," I said, digging my elbow into his side.

"I don't have to be modest," he argued, still grinning easily. "I know my worth—great body, good looks, adoring girlfriend. Man, I've got it all."

"And I happen to know that your great body has one terrible weakness," I said, releasing his hand. "It can't stand being tickled." I attacked his side. He collapsed instantly.

"Don't, Justine. Stop it! Justine, everyone can see us. Help! Jus, that's not fair. I've just played my heart out on a basketball court."

I stopped, reluctantly, still shaking with laughter as he straightened up. "You just wait. You're going to get it. I'll come to your tryouts and tickle you," he said reproachfully.

"I'm not ticklish."

"Then I'll come and strip off my shirt and distract you with my manly body when you're trying to serve."

"I won't even notice. I'm such a great tennis player, you could do your worst and I'd still look good."

"Now who's being modest?" he demanded. "You really think you're good?"

"We'll see tomorrow."

"We have our first practice tomorrow too, at ten-thirty," he said.

"Ours is nine. That's not fair. How come boys get to sleep in and girls have to get up early?"

"Because guys need to conserve their superior strength," he said.

"Huh! Macho jerk," I snapped. "Maybe they want to give the girls the coolest time of day and they don't care if the boys die of heatstroke."

"We're tough. We can take it," he said, laughing. "Anyone who's been through football and soccer training in August can take anything."

"I guess that's true," I agreed. I'd watched Danny play soccer when the temperature was over a hundred degrees.

"Like I said, we men are tough."

"Shut up about you men. There are some very wimpy guys in our grade."

46

"No kidding," he said. "It's pretty bad when I'm the third tallest on the basketball team."

We had reached the parking lot. Cars were starting up and driving away as more and more people left the game. I saw my dad's Mercedes, and I heard him start the engine.

"I guess I have to go," I said slowly. Even though I was comfortable with Danny, I still felt awkward about making plans for after the game.

"Good luck tomorrow," he said. "Thanks for coming to my games all season. It means a lot to me." He reached out and ruffled my hair.

"No problem," I said. "I like watching you be the star."

"Some star," he growled. "Let's hope tennis is better." He paused, kicking a stone across the parking lot. Then he said, "I wish we could do something tonight, but I promised I'd get home early enough to help my mother. We have one of our big family get-togethers tomorrow night. We've got my uncle Dino and my cousin Dominic coming."

"From Italy?" I asked.

He laughed. "From Tucson," he said. "But you'd think you were back in the old country when they're all sitting around the table. Talking, fighting, singing—you can't believe how loud they are. Talk about embarrassing."

He looked at me and squeezed my hand, wanting

47

me to understand. I smiled back, even though I'd never been to a big family gathering and I couldn't imagine what it would be like.

"Hey, tell you what," he said. "Do you want to do something after my practice tomorrow? It's over at noon. We could maybe take in a movie or something before I have to show up at home."

"Sure, that would be great."

"Okay. Do you want to hang around at school and watch our practice?"

"Only if you get up at nine to watch mine."

"No way. What do you think I am? I'll come over to your house."

"Sounds good, Danny. See you tomorrow."

He pulled me close and gave me the sort of kiss that was okay with my father watching.

"Bye," he said. Then he threw his jacket over his shoulder and strolled off to his father's car. Before he got in he looked back and blew me a kiss. I blew him one back and grinned as I got into the car. This friendship with Danny was still like a miracle to me. I had never dreamed that I could be comfortable with a boy. Before this I'd always planned out every sentence I was going to say, blushed when a guy looked at me, and generally acted like a total moron. But Danny was so friendly that it was impossible not to feel at ease with him.

"I'm so lucky," I told my father as we drove away. He just rolled his eyes. He still wasn't used to the idea of his little princess dating. I looked out the window and sighed happily. Danny and I would be playing the same sport, seeing a lot more of each other, getting to know each other even better. I couldn't wait for tennis to start.

Chapter

4

On Saturday morning, when I headed for the tennis courts with my racket in my hand, I wasn't feeling quite so confident. Thanks to my wicked-witch stepmother, I didn't even have a cute new outfit to boost my morale. Now I had to face the tryouts with no designer tennis skirt, and it made me feel insecure.

A whole bunch of girls was already waiting outside the tennis courts. They looked big and strong and confident, and they were all wearing skirts. I could feel my panic rising. Was I really as good as I had thought at tennis? After all, Sagebrush was a small school. I had been one of the best among seventy-five girls. But among three thousand? I pictured what it would be like to have to face my friends if I didn't make the team.

They'd feel sorry for me, and I hate that. I don't like to be pitied.

I took the cover off my racket and walked out onto the court. There were a few girls there already. I recognized a couple of them as basketball standouts. They were also glamour queens—perfect makeup, nice hair, red nails, and very cute tennis outfits. I was horribly conscious of my pink-and-white shorts. I could almost feel them nudging each other and laughing at me, but I was determined to start off by being friendly. That's what my friends were always telling me to do.

"Hi," I called. "Do you guys want to warm up a little?"

They acted like they didn't hear me and swept right past. There were eight of them, and they took the two courts. Then they began hitting back and forth as if I were totally invisible.

"Hey," I wanted to say. "I was on here first. I was going to practice my serves."

But I didn't have the nerve. I just moved to the side and waited for the coach to appear. She came almost immediately—a distinguished looking gray-haired woman, still lean and mean, who looked as if she might have been a top athlete once. She blew a whistle and called us around her.

"I am Ms. Hamilton," she said. "I want varsity girls on this side of me. Frosh-soph on the other side." I moved across with a group of smaller girls. And when I say smaller, I mean *smaller*. *Did I turn into a giant suddenly?* I asked myself. *Are they letting third-graders on the team?* Because that's what most of the other frosh girls looked like. They also looked as if they couldn't play tennis worth diddly.

"I don't think I need to see my returning varsity players right now," she went on, "so if you girls could help me organize?" The glamour queens smiled and stepped aside while she took names and assigned the rest of us to courts. I got put with what looked like the three worst girls in the bunch. There was no way I was going to play with them! I'd be totally doomed.

I was just about to open my mouth and blurt out that I didn't want to be stuck with a bunch of losers, when I forced myself to close it again. *Shut up, Justine,* I told myself firmly. *You don't want to make enemies before you start, do you?* You see how I was learning? A few months ago I'd have stamped my foot and refused to play with them. All the same, I still wasn't thrilled about having to play with munchkins.

We went onto our assigned court. A little chubby girl came and stood beside me. "I'm not too hot at this," she whispered. "I'm only trying out because my mother lives for tennis."

I picked up one of the balls on the court and sent it

over the net. The girl opposite ran forward, missed the ball totally, and crashed into the net. "Sorry," she said.

The other opponent sent a ball across to us. I was about to return it with a nice, smooth forehand, but my partner ran in, swiped at it, and sent it clear over the wire fence.

"Whoops," she said with a giggle.

I had to stop myself from using my racket as a lethal weapon. After ten minutes we hadn't had one rally, and I knew I looked as bad as they did.

"I guess we've seen enough of this group," my glamour queen supervisor said as Ms. Hamilton came along. "All very much beginner level."

To my horror, Ms. Hamilton began to walk off the court with the glamour queen. "Let's bring out four more, Chrissy," I heard her say.

I'd had enough for one morning. I'd been quiet and polite and modest and totally unlike myself, and it hadn't worked.

"Excuse me," I yelled after them.

They turned back to look at me. "You didn't get a fair look at me," I said.

"Oh, I think—" Chrissy began, but I cut in.

"I'm not beginner level. I just got stuck with three people who can't hit the ball."

Ms. Hamilton's expression didn't change. She looked

at me for a moment. Then she said, "Very well. Let's see you rally with Chrissy here."

The glamour queen looked surprised, but she picked up her racket and walked onto the court with me. As she passed her friends I saw her give them a smirk. I knew she was thinking, I'm going to show this little squirt.

Chrissy sent the ball whizzing across as hard as she could, about half an inch over the net. I was too angry to think properly. I just whammed it back at her. As it bounced at her feet, she looked surprised.

"Nice shot," she said grudgingly.

As we went on, I noticed something. She was playing her heart out. She was hitting at me with all her strength, and I wasn't really trying that hard at all. Maybe all those drills at the tennis camps were finally paying off. Maybe the standard at Sagebrush was pretty darned high.

"Let's see you play a couple of games," Ms. Hamilton called. "What's your name, dear?"

"Justine," I said.

"Justine. You serve first."

I served. I have to admit there was a little luck involved. I hadn't meant it to kick out at such an angle, but it was a clear ace. Out of the corner of my eye I could see that a crowd had gathered to watch us. I saw

Chrissy frown. My heart was racing as I served the second time, then the third and fourth. I won the game in straight points.

I looked up to see Ms. Hamilton talking with a tanned, outdoorsy-looking young guy in white shorts. He was watching me with interest. He was also kind of cute. A little too old for me, of course, but definitely cute. Knowing a cute guy was watching made me play even harder. If that girl across the net already hated me, then it didn't make any difference, did it?

At the end of the next game Ms. Hamilton called me across. "You're a good player, Justine," she said. "I'm afraid our freshman team is almost entirely novices this year. I could move you up to varsity, but I have plenty of strong seniors and I've never felt it was fair to push them off a team in favor of an underclassman."

I nodded. I could imagine how I'd be treated by the glamour queens if I pushed one of them off the team. But I couldn't help smiling to myself. She thought I was good enough for varsity!

"I want you to meet Don Schuler," she went on, indicating the cute guy. "He is the boys' tennis coach this year."

"Oh. Hi," I said.

"Nice play out there," he said. "Good hard serve, too. You hit like a guy. I don't think you're going to find much competition in our league. The real strength is in the private school league. Most of the great athletes in the public schools seem to go out for baseball or softball. I've never understood why."

"Me neither," I said. "They seem like wimpy games to me."

He laughed. "I wouldn't say that too loudly around baseball players," he said. "Listen, Justine. Ms. Hamilton asked me to take a look at you because she knew my team was in trouble this year."

I looked up, surprised. Until now it had been polite conversation between strangers. What was he getting at?

"It's clear that you're way ahead of the other freshman girls. Maybe they could learn a lot from you during the season, but I could really use you."

"Excuse me?"

"What I'm saying, Justine, is that I could use you on my guys' team. I've got a couple of strong players, but the rest . . . well, the rest are really weak. I think you'd be well up to standard, and the psychology of having to compete with a girl would make the others work harder, too."

"You want me to play on the guys' team? Is that allowed?"

"Oh sure. Girls can always play on guys' teams. Just not the other way around. We've got a couple of girls in the league who play boys' baseball rather than softball, and they're good, too. And we've had girl tennis players before. So how about it? Do you want to give it a try?"

A big smile was spreading across my face. I'd be playing tennis with Danny—going in the bus with him to away games, sharing secret jokes as we played. . . . And everyone would know who I was—the girl who's so good that she plays on the guys' team! I could just hear the whispers going around school. Finally I'd be a celebrity.

"I'd love to, Mr. Schuler," I said.

"Just call me Don," he said with a grin. "I'm a real easygoing guy, until any of my players disobey me. Then I can turn nasty in a hurry. Just remember that."

"Okay, Don."

"So could you stay on for the boys' practice this morning and meet your teammates?" he asked.

"Sure. No problem," I said.

"Great. See you in a little while, then. Go get something to drink and rest up now. I work my players pretty hard." He patted my shoulder and left.

"Justine! Come over here. We need a fourth," one of the girls called.

"She can't. She's joining the guys' team. She's too good for us," someone else yelled back.

I saw their faces. They thought I was a stuck-up snob. But for once in my life, none of this was my fault. I couldn't help it if I played better than them and the guys' team needed an extra player. To tell you the truth,

I was glad that I was going, and that I didn't have to put up with these snobby girls all season. Instead I'd be playing with Danny and a bunch of fun guys. This would be the greatest experience ever! I couldn't wait to tell Roni, Ginger, and Karen—they'd die with envy! They could keep their boring old track team.

I went into the cool locker room and took a long drink of water, and then I redid my ponytail before coming out to the courts for the guys' practice. I could hear the satisfying thwack of balls as some of the players warmed up. The varsity team on the far courts looked pretty good. That ball was whizzing back and forth so fast I could hardly see it. I was glad I didn't have to play with them!

As for the frosh-soph team . . . well, it was clear they could use some help. Most of the guys were very small. Were we a year of midgets or just late growers? Then I saw Danny's neat, dark hair as he darted across the court. I'd watched him play soccer and basketball, so I knew how well he moved. He hit the ball well, too. Good. I wouldn't have wanted him to be one of the lame ones.

Play came to a halt as I pushed open the gate and stepped onto the court.

"Justine! You hung around after all to watch my practice. That was so sweet of you," Danny said. "Guys, this is Justine. She just got done with her practice. Grab a seat. We're just warming up right now."

I didn't know what to say. I was feeling suddenly shy. "I'm . . . uh . . . here because your coach asked me to be," I said.

"What does he want to do, try to distract us with a girl?" asked the guy playing with Danny.

"Not exactly," I said. "He sort of wanted me to work out with you guys."

"What for?"

"To join your team."

This produced laughter. "Good one, Justine. I thought I was the kidder," Danny said.

"No, seriously. He asked me to come play with you guys. He thought you needed some help."

"Yeah, right. Nice try," Danny said. "Now you better get off the court, or the coach will be mad at us for not playing."

I didn't know what to do, but before I had to make a decision, Don appeared. "Good, you've already met," he said. "You want to take Sam's place on this court, Justine?"

"What is this, Coach?" Danny demanded.

"Oh, I thought you knew. I asked Justine to come over from the girls' team and play with you guys."

"You what?" Danny wasn't smiling now. He turned

to me. "You were serious? He really does want you to play with us?"

I nodded.

"Oh, come off it, Coach. You're putting us on, right? You want us to think that if we don't work hard, even a girl will be able to beat us."

"I think Justine could beat any of you right now," Don said. "That's why I asked her to join. We need strength, and she's a great player."

"For a girl, yes," Danny said, looking at me as if he'd never seen me before.

"Why don't you four warm up a little," Don said, and he started to walk away.

"Okay!" Danny said, giving his partner a smirk. I'd seen that look before. It meant, "Watch out, I'm going to hit my hardest ball, right at you." So I was ready. The ball came over pretty hard, but not as hard as I'd expected. I was able to wham it right back. Then Danny was the surprised one. He'd started to come in to net, and the ball caught him at his feet. He managed a lame scoop to get it back over the net, and I had to stop myself from coming in to finish that one off, too. Danny's partner frowned at me.

I could see I was going to have to play it cool, to get them to respect me and to see that I'd be an asset to the team. I didn't want to bruise their egos. Especially

Danny. I couldn't understand why he was acting like this. I thought he'd be happy to see me. After all, I was happy at the thought of spending so much time with him. But he was behaving in a totally juvenile way. Every shot I hit back to him he seemed to take as a personal insult. When we started to play for points he queried every one of my calls.

"Hey, that service was in by a mile! I could see it."

"Yeah, but you're not the one to call it. I saw it out."

"Okay, if you want to win by cheating!"

"I have to call it like I see it," I said.

My partner looked confused, as if he wasn't sure whose side he was supposed to be on. "It was out, Danny. I saw it too," he said finally.

"Traitor!" Danny muttered. The kind of thing an eight-year-old would say.

By the time Don came over to watch us, Danny was trying so hard to hit winners against me that he was making loads of errors. I started to feel really bad. I had just wanted to join a tennis team, not make everyone unhappy. I knew that, in the past, I had said thoughtless things and behaved in a spoiled way. But now I was really trying to be nice and it was turning out all wrong! I hadn't asked for any of this. So why was Danny, of all people, not able to handle it?

Chapter

5

After a grueling hour and a half, the coach stopped us. "Good first practice," he said. "I can see we've got a long way to go, but there's a lot of potential here. Justine's got the idea of match strategy, but the rest of you have a lot to learn."

"Justine! Coach's pet," I heard one of the guys behind me mimic Don's voice. "I wonder what she had to do to get on the team?"

Dumb giggles followed.

"I hope you guys are going to make an effort to get along well with Justine," Don said firmly. "It isn't easy for her to be the only girl on the guys' team, so don't pull any of your usual dumb stuff, understand me?"

He stalked off ahead of us. I followed with the guys.

As soon as Don was out of earshot, Danny's partner Roger said, "Hey, what happens when we go to away games? Is she going to have to use the guys' locker room? What if we play a game at an all-boys' school?"

More stupid giggles.

"Do you think we'll have to take breaks for broken nails?" Marshall, my partner, chuckled.

"Have to forfeit on bad hair days?" someone else suggested.

I spun around. "You guys are being so childish," I said. "Look, I didn't want to be on this team. I'm doing the coach a favor, that's all. It's not my fault that I'm better than you, so give me a break!"

"Chill, Justine," Danny said. "Everyone on guys' teams kids around. You'll just have to take it, if you want to play with us."

"I don't understand what's gotten into you," I said, looking at him directly. "I thought you'd be happy to have me out here with you. I thought it would be something we could share."

"I like to have you around," he said slowly, "but not like this. Guys' teams are . . . well, a guy kind of thing. A bonding thing, Justine. All guys together, laughing and kidding around. Having you there will just screw things up."

"Gee, I'm glad to know you can't wait to be away from me. That makes me feel real cherished."

"There's a time and a place for everything, Justine," he said. "I like having you as my girl. I like going out on dates with you."

"You used to like me to come to your games," I reminded him.

"Sure, but you're supposed to sit and cheer for me, not try to make me look stupid."

I could feel the color rising in my cheeks. "Oh, I get it," I snapped. "Girls are supposed to sit and cheer while guys are jocks. Is that it?"

"Something like that," he muttered.

"You really believe that?" I yelled.

"Girls can be cheerleaders, or go out for their own stuff, but they have no business trying to compete with guys. It just humiliates us." Danny glared at me angrily. "How do you think it's going to look around school? People will say, 'There goes Danny—you know, the one who has to play second fiddle to his girlfriend!'"

"Well, at least you admit I'm better than you," I said coldly.

"No way. I was just upset today. You completely threw me, showing up like that in front of my friends. It's just not fair to me, Justine."

"I'm sorry," I said. "I didn't realize that the whole world had to revolve around you. I thought we were an equal partnership, Danny, but I see I was wrong. It has to be Danny the hero and Justine cheering for him, or you can't take it."

I turned away and made my grand exit to the girls' locker room. It was only when I was inside, alone in the cool half-darkness, that I realized we were supposed to be going to the movies this afternoon. What happened now?

By the time I had changed and come out of the locker room, there was no sign of Danny or any of the guys. I walked home, my mind in turmoil. I wanted to be a tennis star, but I didn't want to lose Danny. I knew he'd acted like a jerk today, but we'd had such a great time together until now. He was my first real boyfriend. He'd given me my first real kiss. He'd made me laugh and made me feel so special. How could he shoot all that down in one stupid morning?

As soon as I got home I called Roni. "Listen, do you guys want to come over later this afternoon? I could really use the company. We could sit in the spa."

"I thought you and Danny had plans," she said.

"Not anymore."

"Justine, what happened?"

"It's too complicated to talk about over the phone," I said. "Can you come over?"

"I'll call the others and see," she said. "We were going to go shopping, but I'm sure we can cancel that, if you need us, which it sounds like you do. Then we can all go over to Ginger's house together later."

I paced around the empty house, too tense to do anything. My father and stepmother were away for the weekend at a convention in Las Vegas, and they'd already given me permission to spend the night over at Ginger's house. The Saturday night sleepover had become a ritual since the school year began. It was at our first sleepover that the whole Boyfriend Club idea got started. *Dumb Boyfriend Club,* I thought now. A lot of good it had done me, getting me together with Danny! I just hoped my friends would be able to come up with a magic way out of this one!

I was glad my parents were away. Otherwise my father would have quizzed me about my tennis. He was a sports freak, and the only time he really showed any interest in me was when I was succeeding in some kind of sport. I knew he'd latch on to this tennis team thing and brag about it to all his buddies at the golf club: "My little girl was too good for the girls' team so they asked her to show the guys how to play. How about that, eh?"

He'd be proud of me. He might even come to watch my games, which he'd never done before. It was exactly what I'd dreamed of, only now the dream was turning into a nightmare.

All afternoon I waited for the phone to ring. I expected to hear Danny's voice on the other end, apologizing. Then we'd laugh and make up and everything would be the way it was before. But the afternoon went by, and he didn't call. Around four o'clock my friends arrived.

"You sounded so depressed, we stopped off and got a dozen donuts," Roni said, handing me the box. "I know you like the jelly ones."

"Thanks," I said. "I'm so glad to see you guys. I was going bananas on my own."

"What happened?" Karen asked gently. "Did you find that you didn't make the squad after all?"

"Worse than that," I said. "The boys' coach wanted me for his team."

Three faces looked very surprised.

"Run that by me again," Roni said.

"The coaches thought I was too good for the freshman girls and the guys' team could use some help."

"You're not making this up, are you, Justine?" Ginger said slowly. "I mean, you have been known to come up with some very . . . uh . . . creative excuses in your life. If you didn't make the team, come right out and say it."

"I'm telling the truth, guys," I snapped. My nerves were stretched to the breaking point by now. "If you don't believe me, go call the coach. Go ask Danny. I'm sure he'd be happy to tell you all the gory details."

"Hey, Justine, way to go," Ginger said. "I love it.

Justine whips the guys." She made a fist and danced around.

"It's not as great as you think," I said. "Danny's on that team, and he behaved like a kindergartner. He totally freaked out. It was like he felt really threatened."

"Danny?" My friends looked surprised again. "Easygoing, laugh-a-minute Danny? I can't believe it," Roni said. "I would have thought that Danny would think it was funny having a girl on his team."

"Maybe another girl, but not me," I said, blinking back my tears. "He says he'll be the laughingstock of the school, humiliated by his girlfriend."

"What a jerk," Ginger said. "What is it with guys? He probably only wants a girl to adore him and cheer for him. I'm glad you found out before you got too involved with him, Justine."

"That's just the point, I don't want to lose him," I said with a deep, heartfelt sigh. "I really liked him until now. He was so much fun. Now I'm totally confused. I mean, I don't want to give up my chance to play tennis on the guys' team either."

"Of course you shouldn't give it up," Ginger said angrily. "You'd be letting down every girl who dreams of making a major breakthrough in sports. It will be educating a lot of guys when they see that a girl can play as well as them."

"Actually I'm better than most of the freshman guys on the team," I said.

"So there you are. The team needs you, and if Danny can't handle it, then too bad."

"Too bad for me," I said. "We'll break up and I'll never have another boyfriend like him."

"Let's go into the hot tub and eat donuts and think about this," Karen suggested.

"Karen always has the best ideas," Roni said, already heading for the stairs and my bedroom. "Where are your folks today—away again?"

"Yeah, a convention in Las Vegas."

"Sounds like a tough assignment!"

"It is for my stepmom," I said. "She gets tired really easily now, and she hates being in crowds. She's planning to stay in her room all weekend except for meals."

"Poor thing. I don't think I'd like to face Las Vegas if I were pregnant," Roni said. "How many more months?"

"Three."

"Wow," Karen said. "Three more months and you'll be a big sister. Aren't you excited?"

"Sometimes," I said. "Sometimes I can't wait, and then I get all nervous again. I wonder if they'll forget all about me the moment the baby arrives."

"Don't be dumb, of course they won't," Ginger said. "And the baby will adore you. He or she will always look up to you and admire everything you do."

I laughed bitterly. "Which is more than my boyfriend does," I said.

I put on my new black bikini and led my friends down to our spa. Roni remembered to grab the donut box, and for a time we lay back, letting the bubbles relax us while we worked our way through a dozen donuts.

"It was a good idea to eat these in the spa," I said. "I've never learned to eat jelly donuts without the middle squirting out all over me."

"And I've never learned to handle powdered donuts without the powder flying everywhere," Ginger agreed. "We've made quite a mess of your spa."

"I hope we haven't clogged your filter system, or you'll get in trouble," Karen said, looking anxiously at the white sugar floating on the surface.

"Don't worry, it will melt eventually," I said. "And the water will taste sweet for the next few days."

We giggled. Then Karen, suddenly serious, said, "You know, I've been thinking about Danny. It all makes sense when you think about it."

"What does? Acting like a jerk?" Ginger demanded.

"No, feeling threatened by Justine. I mean, he's grown up in a very old-fashioned household. You've been to enough meals there, Justine. His father is the old-time head of the family, isn't he? He and Danny sit at the table while Danny's mom waits on them. She does all the cooking. She's never worked outside the home. So this is how Danny expects women to be. He sees us in support roles."

"Then he'd better learn quickly," Ginger said. "Justine's role in life is not going to be standing on the sidelines and cheering when he scores a goal or serves an ace."

"We should never have started off on the wrong foot," Roni said thoughtfully. "We all started the year by going to watch all the guys' football games. I went to every one of Drew's games when I was dating him, and Ginger went to all of Ben's games."

"But Ben isn't like Danny," Ginger said hastily. "I'm sure he wouldn't feel threatened by a girl on his team. He'd be proud of anything I achieved."

"And James really respects that I need time to practice my violin," Karen said, "and he's very proud when I give a recital."

"It seems to be the macho guys who are most upset by girls succeeding," Roni said. "By the way, you haven't heard the latest on Drew and Cammy yet, have you?"

"I haven't talked to Ben about it yet," Ginger said.

"And I had enough to worry about," I added.

Roni nodded. "You sure did. It's okay. I guess I can wait until Monday."

"You really want to get back together with him, after all he put you through?" Ginger asked her.

Roni sighed. "I don't know. I had so much fun with him. And it was great being his girlfriend."

"But it was also hard being the adoring fan of the star, wasn't it?" Karen reminded her. "You told us you always had to stop and think what you were going to say so that you didn't look like a dope. That's no way to live."

"And I can't see Drew being happy if you turn out to be a track star," I said. "He'd be worse than Danny."

"I'm hardly likely to be a track star."

"You looked pretty good at practice, Roni," Karen said.

"And you looked amazing," Roni returned. "I can't believe the way you go over that high jump."

"I can't either," Karen agreed. "It just seems to work."

"And Ginger looked like she was winning most of the sprints," Roni said. "Who would have thought we'd turn out to be four jockettes?"

I sighed again. "Who would have thought that being a jockette would produce such big headaches?" I said. "What am I going to do, guys?"

"I think you should hang in there," Ginger said. "If Danny can't learn to handle your success, then he wasn't the right guy for you anyway."

"But I think he'll mellow out after he gets used to it," Roni said. "I mean, he's usually such a cool guy. I really can't see him stomping off the team because he has to play with a girl. That's a very uncool thing to do."

"I agree," Karen said. "I think you took him by surprise today, Justine. I bet he's at home right now, feeling bad about the way he acted this morning. On Monday I bet he'll be his old sweet, funny self, as if today never happened."

"You really think so?" I asked hopefully.

"Sure," Karen agreed, "Danny is a sweet, thoughtful guy. Look how he rescued you from that snobby sorority that time. He cares about you, Justine. He's not going to let a little thing like a tennis team stand in the way of your friendship."

I lay back and looked at the palm leaves swaying above my head. I began to feel more hopeful. Maybe I had made too big a deal of this morning's fiasco. Danny had been shocked and taken by surprise. Anyone would react badly when they'd been upset. He'd see the funny side by now. When we met again, he'd be joking about it.

"I hope you're right," I said.

Chapter

6

I didn't talk to Danny on Monday until I went out to the courts for afternoon practice, but the news about my playing on the boys' team had sure spread all over the school. Kids stopped me in the halls and asked me if I was the one. Most of the girls seemed really excited for me, except for a couple of my former teammates on the frosh girls' team. In the locker room before practice, I heard one of them telling her friends about me. "Everyone on our team wanted to get rid of her, anyway," she sniffed. "She was a show-off."

I wanted to spin around and tell them that this just wasn't true, but I took a deep breath and pretended I hadn't even heard. They were just jealous.

I had given a lot of thought to what to wear to practice. No more little pink-and-white matching outfits, if I didn't want to get teased. I found a pair of plain white shorts at the back of my closet and a blue-and-white striped shirt that looked un-girly and businesslike. From now on I'd be one of the guys. No more jokes about broken fingernails.

Two of the boys looked up as they heard me open the gate to the courts.

"Oh, look, it's Tinkerbell," one said.

"What happened to the pink-and-white outfit?"

"She lost the matching hair ribbon!"

I ignored them both and walked over to put my racket cover down on the bench. I looked up to see Danny standing beside me. For a second my heart jumped. He wanted to apologize after all. I gave him an encouraging smile.

"Hi," I said.

"Justine, I have to talk to you before we start playing," he muttered.

"Sure."

"I've been thinking about this all weekend and I have to tell you that I still don't think it's a good idea. I was hoping that you'd decided the same thing, for both our sakes."

"I really don't see that there's a major problem, Danny," I said. I could feel my smile wavering.

"If you were any other girl, it would probably have been okay. But not my girlfriend, Justine. I can't handle playing on the same team as you."

I did my best to stare at him coldly. "What you're saying is that you want me to quit?"

I could see the relief flood over Danny's face. "It's the only way, Jus. I mean, this isn't fair to me. You're distracting me. You're putting me off my game."

I took a deep breath to compose myself. I was not going to make a scene. I wasn't going to let Danny see how much he was upsetting me.

"And what about *my* game? Don't I have a right to make the best of my tennis?"

"Sure you do, Justine, only not here. Not with me. Not if you care about us." He paused and looked at me with pained eyes. "There's a girls' team you could play on, where you belong. You'd be the star. You'd have a great time. Why don't you quit right now and let things get back to where they were, Justine?"

I couldn't believe he was saying these things. I didn't know what to do.

"Because I don't think our relationship can take this stress," Danny continued. "If you keep playing here, then it's all over between us."

I felt a big jolt of panic. Did I want things to be all over between us? This was Danny—the guy I had

76

dreamed of all my life, my funny, warm, caring Danny. And he was behaving like a stranger.

"I don't see why you're so threatened by me," I said. "I don't see why you're acting like a ten-year-old, whining that it's not fair."

"Well, it's not," he retorted. "You're wrecking my chances here. You have another team you could be on, but I can't join the girls' team—they wouldn't let me. So it's not fair, is it?"

"I think you're really worried that I'll be better than you, that you'll have to play second fiddle to a girl."

"Huh," he snapped. "I could beat the pants off you."

"Then prove it. I'm only here to play tennis. Just pretend I don't exist and . . . and I'll do the same." It was probably the hardest thing I'd ever said in my life.

"Quit the chatting and get on with warming up," the coach yelled. "I want to make some preliminary decisions about who plays singles and who plays doubles today. I want to see you play under match conditions."

I walked over onto another court and warmed up with three wimpy freshmen. I didn't get much of a warm-up, because most of the balls I sent over the net didn't come back. After half an hour the coach called us all together.

"I want the following players to go onto courts one and two to play singles," he said. "Hal and Marshall on court one, and Danny and Justine on court two."

Before I could react to this, Danny stepped forward. "Look, Coach, couldn't I play on the other court with Marshall and let her play Hal? He's the best player on the team, after all. Let's see if she can beat him."

The coach's eyes narrowed, but he merely said, "If you want to be on this team, Pandini, don't question my orders. When I say jump, you say how high. Got it?"

"Yessir," Danny mumbled. He glared at me as he headed for the court, as if this were all my fault.

Marshall and Hal took their places on the court beside us and immediately began rallying. I noted that Hal was, as Danny had said, pretty good. He was also taller and older looking than the other guys. *Must be a sophomore,* I thought, *and not bad-looking, either.* I switched my attention back to Danny, who was glaring at me from across the court. As soon as I was in position, he began hitting balls as hard as he could, putting all his anger into them. When I came in to net he hit a ball right at me, making me jump aside with my racket in front of my body.

He grinned. "If you play with the guys, you're going to have to learn to play hardball," he said.

"That's okay. It's a shot I'd do myself," I said, trying to sound calmer than I really was. "Only I wouldn't waste it in warm-up. There are just certain ethics of the game, which I suppose *you* wouldn't know, being a beginner."

"Score Justine fifteen, Danny love," I muttered to myself as I walked back again. Danny—love. Sure! There had been real love between Danny and me, and now suddenly we were acting like enemies. It didn't make sense. How could you love a person one minute and want to hurt them the next? I wanted to grab Danny by the shoulders and shake sense into him. "Why are we letting this stupid thing spoil something sweet and wonderful?" I wanted to shout. This is dumb!

"Begin play," the coach called. "Craft to serve."

I walked to the service line and juggled the balls in my hand. I could solve this right away. I could make everything the way it was. All I had to do was to play badly enough that the coach didn't want me on the team. I could let him think that I cracked during a match situation, that I couldn't handle pressure. Then I could go back to the girls' team, and Danny would like me again.

I served into the net.

"Fault," the coach called.

I served again. Wide this time.

"Double fault. Love-fifteen."

I saw Danny's grin and I read what it meant. "I've made her so rattled that she can't play. I've psyched her out." Suddenly I knew that Danny didn't care at all about my feelings. If I left the court completely humiliated, if I had gotten hit with a ball and started to cry, he wouldn't have cared. He would have gotten rid of an embarrassment and left himself as king of the court again. This was supposed to be the most important person in my life. And all the time he had only really cared about himself.

I walked across to the ad court and bounced a ball while I composed my thoughts. Okay, so it was going to be war. Well, I'd show him that he couldn't make me quit, whatever he did. I had a right to be on this team. I was good enough and I was tough enough . . . and I was a better player than he was!

I tossed the ball and served. The serve was hard and right down the center line. Danny didn't even move for it.

"Fifteen all," the coach called.

Danny's face turned bright red. "That ball was out!" he yelled. "It was way out. Anyone could see that."

The coach looked at him coldly. "Two things, Pandini. Number one, it was an exceptionally good serve, right down the center line. It aced you. You should have the grace to admit when a shot is too good for you. And number two, I am umpiring this game. When I give a call, you do not dispute it *ever*. Understand me?"

Danny muttered something and stomped over to the

other side of the court. Play continued. It wasn't hard to beat him, because now he was psyching himself out. He was so mad at Don and at me that he was trying impossibly hard serves, coming in to finish off shots he couldn't finish and letting me pass him left and right. The more mistakes he made, the madder he got.

When there was another close call, he took a ball and whammed it up into the sky, out over the court netting.

Don stopped play and called us over. "Danny," he said. "If you can't control your temper, then this game isn't for you. And we don't have the kind of budget that lets us lose balls."

"I can play just fine if the other person is playing fair," Danny stormed. "She's hitting all these stupid trick shots and you keep calling her balls in when they're out. You're falling over backward to make her look good and me look bad."

Don frowned. "I've always been totally fair to all my players," he said. "And in this case I wouldn't have to try to make you look bad. You're making yourself look bad enough without my help."

"I play better than this," Danny yelled. "It's just that playing against a girl is putting me off. I can't concentrate."

"Because of her sexy body? Give me a break, Danny," the coach said. "Let's get one thing straight. If you can't handle being on this team, then quit right now and let someone else take your place. Someone who *does* want to be here."

Danny's face was beet red by now. "I do want to be here," he said. "I want to be on a guys' team, with other guys, not with a coach who has some harebrained idea about giving a stupid girl a chance to prove females are equal!"

"She's more than equal. She was beating you pretty badly," Don said, with something close to a grin. "I think she's going to be one of my top singles players. I thought you were, too."

"You know what this is?" Danny yelled. "This is stupid."

"And you know what you are, Danny?" the coach echoed. "You're off the team. I'm not taking this kind of nonsense from any player, however good he is. Pick up your things and get out."

Danny stopped, openmouthed. "You're kicking me off the team? Because of her?"

"No, because of you. Unless you can radically change your attitude, I don't want to see your face again."

"Fine," Danny stormed. "If this is the way tennis is going to be run at this school, then fine. I hope your dumb girl wins matches for you."

He picked up his racket and stormed off the court, slamming the gate so violently that the wire jingled. The rest of us watched in stunned silence. Part of me wanted to run after him and beg him to come back. I wanted to say I was sorry and I hadn't meant to mess up his life. But the other part of me whispered that I hadn't done anything wrong. In fact, for once I was the one who had kept my temper and not acted like a spoiled brat. And look where it had gotten me—I had just lost the only guy I had ever loved.

"Sorry about that, Justine," Don said quietly. "Some guys have very fragile egos. It takes them a while to realize that they don't have to feel threatened by athletic girls."

"You don't understand the whole story, Coach," I said. "Danny and I were dating. That's why he took this so hard. He thought that he'd be teased around school if his girlfriend could beat him at tennis. He's always been a real jock—one of the stars. I guess it's extra hard for him."

Don nodded. "I knew you two were an item," he said. "But that shouldn't make any difference. Plenty of couples have faced each other in mixed doubles tournaments and it doesn't usually affect their play."

"But I feel really bad that Danny is off the team," I said. "He lives for sports. Maybe I should quit. I'm causing so much trouble here."

"Do you want to quit?"

I shook my head firmly. "Oh, no. I really want to play."

"Then play. Your Danny has got a lot of growing up to do. He'll have to learn the hard way. I tell you what—I'll keep him off the team for a week and then I'll give him one more chance. Any more temper tantrums and he's off for good."

"Thanks, Coach," I said.

"Maybe the shock of being kicked off a team will teach him a lesson," Don said. "Let's just hope his pride won't stop him from coming back again. He's got a lot of potential as a player. The team really needs him."

"I wish there was something I could say to make him see how dumb he's being," I said.

Don smiled. "That's something he's got to learn for himself. If he finds out that his pride has lost him both his girl and his place on the team, then maybe he'll start to see sense."

"Maybe," I said, trying to sound more hopeful than I felt.

But when I saw Danny in the parking lot after practice, he walked past me as if I didn't even exist.

Chapter

7

I've felt pretty bad at times during my life. I felt bad each time my father dumped me at a new school and then didn't write or call me. I felt terrible when I had to stand there as a flower girl at his wedding to Christine, and even worse when I found out that they were going to have a baby. But I'd never felt as bad as this before.

It was so unfair. All my life I'd been known for saying dumb things I didn't really mean. I suppose it was even true that I'd boasted just a little . . . from time to time . . . and claimed to be able to do things I really couldn't do at all. But this time I'd done none of the above. I wasn't the one who pushed me onto the guys' team. I wasn't the one who claimed to be the best player. I wasn't even the one who lost my temper and said dumb things. And what had happened? I'd lost my boyfriend, and everyone hated me.

I was lying back, musing about this, under our favorite tree at lunchtime, watching the pattern of clouds changing through the leaves. I wished that somehow everything could be all right again. I knew Danny had behaved like a total creep, but I missed him already. A whole weekend without one of his funny phone calls. A whole day at school without bumping into him in the halls and going to my next class with a big smile on my face.

I could hear my friends talking excitedly beside me, but I couldn't bring myself to join in their conversation. Occasional snatches managed to get through my thick cloud of doom, so I guessed they were talking about Roni and Drew.

"And one girl said that Cammy cried in the middle of math class. Can you imagine how embarrassing that must have been?"

"So they really broke up?"

"This girl said that Drew told Cammy they were never really going together, just hanging out as friends. He said she should have known he gets bored easily."

"That's amazing," I heard Roni's voice. "You're really, truly sure that these girls were talking about Cammy and Drew, not about someone else?"

"I'm sure, Roni," Karen said. "Justine heard them too, didn't you, Justine?"

"What?" I jerked myself back to reality.

"The two girls in the bathroom before we came out here? The ones who were talking about Cammy and Drew."

"I didn't notice any girls," I said, feeling stupid. "Sorry. All I can think about is Danny and tennis and how bad I feel."

"Here, have a brownie," Karen said kindly.

I looked up at the green canopy of leaves and sighed. "No, thanks. I don't feel like eating anything."

"But you have to eat," Karen said, giving me a motherly frown. "And I made the brownies specially to cheer you up, because I know they're your favorite."

"Thanks," I said, managing a halfhearted smile, "but I honestly don't think I could swallow anything. I just feel so bad. Danny hates me, his friends hate me, the girls' tennis team hates me, and the guys wish I weren't there."

"We don't hate you," Karen said. "We feel bad for you. If there was something we could do, other than bake brownies, we would."

"You could wave a magic wand and make it be last week again," I said. "Then I'd never have gone out for the dumb tennis team, and everything would be fine between Danny and me."

My friends exchanged glances.

"It would have had to come to this sometime," Ginger said. "His attitude about women would have spoiled things between you one day. Let's face it, Justine, the guy has attitudes that went out with the pioneers. The first time he wanted you to watch one of his games when you wanted to do something else, he'd have had the same temper tantrum."

"Yeah, Justine," Roni said. "He has to learn that women are not put on this earth to worship men. Until he realizes that we are equal in every way—"

"Yoo hoo, girls!" came Owen's piercing shout. Nerds converged on us, grinning their terrible grins.

"I hope we're not equal to them," Karen muttered under her breath.

"Forget what I just said," Roni agreed as we looked around and saw that there was no chance of escape. "If we're not superior to the nerds, we're doomed."

"We've been looking for you all over," Owen said. "You weren't under this tree last time we looked."

"That was because the ground's been too wet to sit on," Roni said patiently.

"Oh, good point," Owen said, as if this had never occurred to him before. "That's why, Ronald. I'm surprised you couldn't figure it out."

"You thought they'd been zapped up by aliens," Ronald said.

"It was only a suggestion," Owen argued.

We looked at each other. Ginger raised her eyes. "Okay, so what did you want us for?"

"We wanted to talk to you about the Valentine's Dance, of course," Owen said. "We wondered if you all had partners yet, or if you'd like to accompany us."

"Oh, gee, I'm sorry, but we all have dates already," Karen said quickly.

"I don't have a—" I began, but Roni dug me in the ribs.

"Sure you do," she said.

"I suppose you'll be going with our good buddy Chris, right, Roni?" Owen asked.

"Chris?" Roni squeaked.

"Yeah. He mentioned that he was getting up the courage to ask you. He's very excited about going to a dance with you."

"Oh . . . yeah, sure, I guess we'll be going together," Roni said.

"But you said . . ." I began. I was confused now. What had she been saying two minutes ago? Hadn't she been excited that Drew had broken up with Cammy? And wasn't she scared Chris might dance like a nerd-octopus-robot?

Roni dug me in the ribs again, so hard that it almost

89

knocked the breath out of me. "Ow," I said.

"We all have dates, guys," Ginger said very firmly, "and we're all going in a big group with my boyfriend Ben and all his football team buddies. You know—the linebackers, all over two hundred pounds?"

"Oh, well, that's that," Ronald said quickly. The nerds had fallen strangely silent. They were probably all thinking about big, strong football types, who tended to enjoy squashing nerds in their spare time.

"Some other time, maybe," Owen said.

"Maybe," Roni said. "In your dreams," she added under her breath as the nerds began to move off.

"Looks like you're stuck going with Chris now," Ginger reminded her.

"What else could I say?" Roni snapped. "If I decide to tell him I'm not going to the dance with him, I certainly don't want him to hear via the nerds. I really like Chris. I don't want to hurt his feelings, just when he's getting some confidence."

"Then I don't see how you can go to the dance with Drew," Karen said. "I'd say that would be a rather impressive blow to his confidence."

Roni sighed. "You're right. I'd feel like a heel. What am I going to do, guys?"

"Go with Chris and then dance with Drew," I said.

The others looked at me. "What?" I demanded. "It

seems like a perfectly simple solution to me."

"She can't just dump Chris," Karen said. "She'll have to decide."

"We don't even know if Drew actually asked her that night at the basketball game," Ginger said. "Was that an invitation, or just friendly conversation?"

"Sounded like an invitation to me," I said. "Boys don't go around talking about dances unless they're inviting you."

Roni sighed again. "This is so complicated," she said. "I don't want to hurt Chris, but I'd love to dance with Drew."

"Maybe the question is really whether you want to get back together with Drew," Karen said. "You can't go to a dance with him and then say no thanks, I have more fun with Chris."

"You're right," Roni said, "and my conscience tells me that I'd feel awful if I dumped Chris. I hated it when Drew dumped me."

"Then go with Chris and just pray he doesn't want to hang out with the nerds all evening," Ginger said.

Roni gave her a horrified look. "He wouldn't do that, would he?"

"It's a possibility," Karen said.

Roni shuddered. "This dance is sounding less and less appealing."

"You just have to keep him away from nerds," I said.

"Keep him on the dance floor all night," Karen said. "Put your head on his shoulder, wrap your arms around him, and keep him trapped there. That's what I plan to do with James, because I know he won't want to stay long. He's already said that he's not exactly thrilled about going, but he'll put in a token appearance, for my sake."

"But what about me?" I asked. "I won't be able to come. And I was really looking forward to it. I even saw the cutest red dress in the store. . . ."

"Sure you'll be able to come," Karen said comfortingly.

"But I don't have a date."

"You can come without a partner. It's not a formal."

"Oh, sure. That will be just dandy," I said. "It will be a blast sitting in a corner, watching all of you dancing with your boyfriends while I'm trying to hide from nerds behind the potted plants."

"Maybe you'll meet a cute new guy," Ginger suggested. "Then you can show that Danny creep that he's not the only guy in the world."

"I don't know," I said. I didn't think it was very likely that I'd meet a cute new guy at a big school dance. Usually those things were such chaos and the music was so loud that it was impossible to meet anyone. Also I wasn't sure that I wanted a new guy. I knew I wasn't over Danny. I didn't know if I ever would be.

"Oh, please come, Justine," Roni said. "You can talk

to Chris and me all night. That will help keep him away from the nerds."

"What if we both get swallowed up into the nerd pack and are never seen again?"

"It's a big dance. Anyway, we'll hang out with Ginger and Ben and the football guys. That'll keep the nerds away."

"What if Danny's there?" I hadn't thought about that before. "And what if he's having a good time without me and he's dancing with another girl? I don't think I could handle it."

"Maybe you could ask another guy, and make Danny insane with jealousy," Karen suggested.

"Get real, Karen. What other guys do I know? Besides, Danny wouldn't even care anymore. He hates my guts."

The bell rang. I got up and grabbed my book bag. "Thanks for trying, guys, but we have to face the fact that my life is over. I'll just have to be a lonely tennis star, walking back from Wimbledon to my empty room. . . ."

I saw them exchange a quick grin as I walked past them to my locker. It was okay for them. They hadn't just lost the love of their lives. They hadn't just had the guy they loved turn on them.

All afternoon I found it hard to concentrate on what the teachers were saying. I thought about what my friends had said. Maybe they were right. Maybe I *should* try to find another guy to take to that dance. I'd show Danny that I could forget about him just as easily as he had forgotten about me! But the only guys I knew were nerds—and I wanted Danny to feel jealousy, not pity. It had to be a drop-dead cute guy or no one at all. And what drop-dead cute guys even knew my name? It was hopeless.

Valentine's Day excitement began to take over the school. Big posters with hearts all over them appeared in all the hallways to publicize the dance. Red paper hearts were stuck all over the walls. There were notices in the daily bulletin about ordering Valentine's surprise roses and candy hearts to be delivered on the big day. Every time another of those announcements came over the PA, I felt a big jolt of misery. What fun it would have been, wondering if Danny was going to send me a candygram or red roses. I could imagine the roses being delivered to my desk and everyone wanting to know who they were from. Now I'd probably be the only person who got nothing for Valentine's Day. I was glad I had tennis practice every afternoon to work off all that anger and disappointment.

Things were going pretty well on the tennis court now that Danny wasn't there. The other players had stopped making dumb jokes about me. A couple of

Danny's friends still glared at me, as if they held me responsible for Danny being kicked off the team. But the rest realized I could play tennis, and they were okay.

I spent most of my time working out with Marshall and Hal, the interesting but quiet sophomore. They were both pretty intense as players, and neither of them said much. I got the feeling that they were both kind of shy around girls and didn't really know what to say to me. That was fine with me. I just wanted to be left alone.

I tried not even to think of the dance or of Danny. I worked so hard on the court that Don told me he had great hopes for me. "Keep on like this, and you might land yourself a scholarship to a good college," he said one day. "You've got real potential, Justine."

Any other time I would have been bursting with pride. Now it didn't even seem to matter. I went back to the locker room and collapsed onto the nearest bench.

"Are you too big a tennis star to say hi to your old friends now, Justine?" a voice said.

"Roni? I didn't see you," I said. She was sitting in the shadows with one shoe off and one shoe on. "Did you just get out of track?"

"A while ago," she said. "The others already left. I've been sitting here, thinking."

"About what?"

"Lots of things, mainly the dance," she said. "I saw

Drew this afternoon. He was working out on the base-ball diamond, and he waved at me as we ran past. He has the world's cutest smile, Justine."

"You still miss him, right?"

She nodded. "Every time I see him I keep reminding myself that I could be back with him if I wanted. And now I've told Chris that he can go ahead and get dance tickets for us when they go on sale. What a mess."

"So you're tired of Chris? You definitely don't want to go to the dance with him?"

"I like him, Justine. I feel so comfortable around him. You know what I mean? I can be myself. With Drew I always felt like I was acting. And I can't back out of the dance now, can I? Not after I've said yes to Chris."

"I don't know," I said. "If it were me, I'd come up with some creative excuse. Can't you send Chris to a nerds' convention in Alaska for the weekend?"

Roni laughed. "Justine, you're something else."

"You have to get rid of him somehow," I said. "I know who I'd rather be seen at the dance with."

"I know too," she said, "but I don't want to hurt Chris. I don't want to lose him, either. He's the only boy I've ever had in my life who is a true friend. It's just that . . ."

"That you're not over Drew yet," I finished for her.

She nodded. "I don't think I'll ever really get over

him. He was my first real boyfriend, my first giant crush."

"Just like Danny," I blurted out. "I don't know if I'll ever truly get over him. I still can't understand it, Roni. One moment everything was perfect, and then suddenly, wham, he's turned into a person I don't even recognize."

"I guess it's hard to understand boys," Roni said. "How can we know what's going on in their heads?"

"But we should know by now," I said. "I mean, I thought I knew Danny . . ."

"Poor Justine," Roni said. "We all know you're hurting about Danny. If we could find some way to make it better for you, we would."

"It would take a miracle," I said with a sigh. "Let's face it, Roni. I found the one true love of my life, and now I've lost him."

Chapter

8

The week before the big dance, I was heading to my locker to get my lunch bag. Since I'd started all this hard work on the tennis court, my appetite was enormous. I could hear my croissant with turkey and Swiss calling to me. But when I came around the corner, I almost ran smack into Ginger and Ben. And they weren't looking too happy.

"Okay, fine, if that's how you want it," she was saying.

"Ginger, don't be like that," he said. "I'd go if I could. I thought you'd understand."

"Oh, I understand," she said icily. "You don't care if we go or not. You'd rather be playing baseball. You'd better hurry, or you might be ten seconds late to your dumb meeting!"

Then she swept past him and grabbed my arm. "Come on, Justine, we're going to get our tickets," Ginger said, dragging me down the hall before I had time to protest.

"What? What tickets?"

"Tickets for the Valentine's Day Dance, dummy. They go on sale today. We want to make sure they don't sell out."

Roni and Karen came running up to join us. They both looked happy and excited. I felt like the Grinch who stole Christmas.

"Don't get me wrong, but aren't guys supposed to take girls to a dance?" I demanded. "I know we're liberated women, but why not let your boyfriends stand in line for tickets?"

"I know," Ginger said, and her smile faded. "Ben was going to get the tickets, but they have a baseball meeting at lunch today, so he asked me if I'd do it. What could I say?"

"And knowing how James is acting about this dance, he might just forget to buy the tickets," Karen said. "He is not enthused, I can tell you. So I'm going to make sure we're going. I'm not about to miss out on a chance to get dressed up and dance with James."

"I'd told Chris he could get our tickets," Roni said. "I hope I'm not making a terrible mistake saying I'd go

99

with him. You guys have got to promise to rescue me from the nerd pack if they show up." She put her arm around my shoulder. "At least I can rely on good old Justine to fight off nerds for me. She knows just the right things to say to make nerds vanish. Right, Justine?"

"I'm not going," I said.

"Justine, you have to!" Karen exclaimed.

"I'm not going by myself," I said. "Sorry, guys, but you'll all have someone. I'll be all alone. You know how I hate people feeling sorry for me."

"You won't be alone, Justine," Karen said. "We'll all hang out together in a big group. We won't let you be a wallflower, we promise."

"I'll stand in line with you," I said grudgingly, "but I'm not coming to the dance. I couldn't handle it if Danny was there with another girl."

"Come on, Justine, please get a ticket," Roni begged. "Pretty please with sugar on top?" And she made such a funny face that I had to laugh. My face felt as if it had moved to a strange new position. I hadn't laughed since Danny and I broke up. When we were together, he was always cracking me up. I missed him so much it hurt. But it hurt even more to realize that he wasn't the funny, nice guy I'd thought he was. *It just shows how little I know about boys,* I decided. I always pretend I'm so sophisticated and experienced, but I'm really not.

Just between you and me, Danny was my first real boy-friend . . . and now he was gone.

We were close to the front of the line when Danny walked past with a group of his friends. He saw me, then pretended he hadn't.

"Hey, Danny, you want to get our tickets?" one of his friends asked.

"Nah, waste of time," Danny said. "Who wants to go to a dumb Valentine's Dance? It will be boring."

"But I thought you liked that kind of stuff," the boy went on.

"I said *no,* Tyler," Danny cut in. "Now drop it."

"Okay, keep your hair on," Tyler said.

I couldn't believe it! Danny didn't want to go to the dance because he thought I'd be there. If he'd gotten over me, he wouldn't have cared if I was going or not. That must mean he still cared a little, even if he didn't want to admit it.

We reached the front of the line. Danny was still hanging around. I guess his friends wanted tickets. I had no alternative. My turn came, and I had to buy a ticket.

"All right, Justine. You did it," Karen said.

"This doesn't mean that I'm coming," I said. "It's just in case I change my mind at the last minute."

But that afternoon, on the way home from tennis

practice, I did stop off at the store with the red dress, and I tried it on, just in case. It looked great on me— not too old, but sexy at the same time. I almost found myself taking out my charge card. Then I thought, *What does it matter what I wear to the dance? There will be nobody there to see me.* That shows you how very depressed I was! Justine, the fashion queen, not caring what she wore?

"So what fantastic weekend plans do we have?" Ginger asked on Friday, as we headed out to eat lunch.

"I was going to suggest that we all go shopping to choose Valentine's Day cards together," Roni said. "And maybe we could just take a look at dresses in case there are any good sales on."

"Yeah, let's do it," Ginger said. "I have absolutely no money to get a new dress, but maybe we can find some cute accessories. Like a red rose for my hair."

"What about Justine?" Karen asked, looking anxiously at me. "It won't be much fun for her watching us get Valentines."

"Don't worry about me, guys," I said. "You go ahead and have a great time. I'll be busy looking into convents. I think I'm just about ready to become a nun."

They all laughed, for some strange reason. "Yeah, Justine, I can just see it," Roni gasped. "Do they have orders with designer habits?"

"It will have to be a convent with a tennis court, and a good teaching pro," Ginger agreed.

"I spent eight years in Catholic schools with fierce power nuns, Justine," Karen said. "They take vows of poverty and obedience."

"Don't they have any rich orders of nuns?" I asked.

"What about obedience, Justine? You have to be humble. It's a sin to brag. When the other sisters tell you you've done something wrong, you have to say 'Thank you for pointing that out, Sister,' not 'Shut up!'"

"I could learn," I said, tossing back my hair. "You should see me on the tennis court. You'd be really proud of me. I take criticism. When the guys make dumb remarks about me, I pretend I haven't heard."

"I hear you're really good," Karen said. "Two guys in my math class were talking about you. They said you're the best one on the team."

"Really?" I felt myself blushing. "But I don't think I'm the best one on the team. Hal's good."

"Hal?"

"He's a sophomore. Not bad looking. Tall, but kind of skinny. Sort of the strong, silent type. He doesn't talk much. I think he's shy. But he's a good tennis player."

"Is Danny still off the team?" Karen asked cautiously.

I nodded. "The coach won't let him come back until

he changes his attitude, and he won't change his attitude while I'm still there."

"That's tough," Ginger said. "I bet he hates not playing. He's such a jock."

"Don't look at me, it's not my fault," I said. "I didn't get him kicked off the team."

"We know that, Justine," Ginger said hastily. "You can't help being a star tennis player."

"We'll see about that tomorrow," I said. "We have our first preseason invitational. I'm not sure how I'll do against other schools that have good tennis programs. You guys want to come and watch? I could use a cheering section."

"We'd love to," Karen began, "but we have our first practice track meet. I'm so nervous. I hope I don't forget how to high jump and land on my fanny."

"You'll do fine," I said. "So are we all coming to my house for the sleepover afterward? Or do you guys have dates?"

"Of course we'll come," Ginger said. "It's tradition. Besides, Ben won't be home from his baseball tournament until late."

"And Chris is going to some sort of computer exhibition with the nerds," Roni said, wrinkling her nose in disgust.

"I thought you had him away from all that by now," I exclaimed.

"I thought so too, but he hates to say no to them," she said.

"James is going to that exhibition, too," Karen added. "He wanted me to come, but I told him I had the track meet."

"You should have made him come and cheer for you," Ginger said firmly. "I would have made Ben if he didn't have a baseball game."

"I think it would have made me nervous knowing he was watching," Karen said. "Besides, I want him to do his own thing. When he's happy, I'm happy."

I looked across at Roni, and we put our fingers down our throats and made gagging noises.

When I opened my locker, an envelope fell out.

"What's that?" Karen asked.

I bent to pick it up. "I have no idea. How did it get in there?"

"Someone must have pushed it through the slats," Ginger said, peering over my shoulder curiously. "Go on, open it."

I opened it. It was a Valentine's Day card, a big, red heart with the words "You make my heart beat faster."

"Someone must have pushed this into the wrong locker," I said to Karen.

Karen was examining the envelope. "It says Justine on the front," she said. "Do you recognize the writing?"

I looked at it and shook my head.

"Well, who's it from?" Roni demanded. "Don't keep us in suspense any longer."

I opened the card. Inside was printed in neat black letters, "Valentine's Day Dance? Be there. From your secret admirer."

"Hey, Justine, how about that!" Karen exclaimed excitedly. "You have a secret admirer."

"It's probably a joke," I said, feeling my cheeks turning bright red.

"It's an expensive card," Roni said, turning it over in her hand. "Too good for a joke. And why would anyone want to play a joke on you?"

"Danny, to get even?"

"From what you said, it sounds as if he's trying to forget all about you, not keep reminding himself," she said.

"Then who?" I looked at the card as if it could tell me.

Roni shrugged. "Someone who likes you and doesn't have the courage to say so."

Suddenly I had a great idea. "Hey, you know what? This is a job for the Boyfriend Club!"

My friends looked at each other and grinned. "How can we help, Justine?"

"Snoop around. Ask questions. Find out who my secret admirer is before I go totally bananas."

"Don't you want the fun of discovering who it is for

106

yourself? What if he keeps on sending cards and every card gives you another clue, and then at the dance he steps from the shadows and—"

"And he might be totally gross!" I yelled. "I need to be prepared. I have to be wearing the right kind of outfit to match his personality. Come on. You can do it. Find out who my secret admirer is before the Valentine's Dance!"

"Okay, we'll try, but we can't promise anything," Karen said. "After all, he might be the shy type."

"Somebody who never had the courage to speak his love for you while Danny was in the picture," Roni added.

"The Phantom of Alta Mesa," Ginger exclaimed.

"Now you see why I need the Boyfriend Club," I said. "I don't want to be dragged down to the bowels of the school and locked in the boiler room by a phantom! You guys have got to find out who he is!"

As I went to my classes, I tried to remember if I'd ever caught any guy watching me. I couldn't think of anyone. The only ones who had shown any active interest in me were the nerds, but there was nothing secret about their admiration. If one of them admired me, he'd come right out and say it. But it was exciting to think that somewhere in this big school a guy actually liked me. A guy who hopefully wasn't a nerd wanted to meet me at the Valentine's Day Dance. I was glad I'd bought the ticket after all. Now I might even buy that dress, if I didn't die of curiosity first.

At tennis practice that day, Marshall said, "So who's going to the Valentine's Dance? Hal?"

And Hal looked at me. "I'm not sure yet. Maybe, if things turn out the way I want. . . ."

I felt a cold shiver go up my spine. Was Hal my secret admirer? That's why I hadn't gotten the feeling of being watched in classes, because Hal was a sophomore. But this was crazy! He'd never shown any indication . . . he treated me like any other tennis player. He'd hardly ever said a word to me except for "Good shot."

Then I thought about some other things. Hal had never teased me like some of the guys did, and he had complimented me on my tennis. And he didn't speak much to anyone. Maybe he was one of those guys who keep their emotions locked away, but love passionately in secret. I snuck another glance at him as he walked back to serve. He was taller than the other guys on the team and good looking in a dark and brooding sort of way. In fact, he looked a little like a poet with serious, haunted eyes. Exactly the kind of guy who would send a girl love letters, or cards with hearts on them!

The ball came flying in my direction, and I missed it completely.

"Keep your eye on the ball, Justine," Don warned. "You never know what those guys on the other side of the net are going to do next." If he'd known what I had been thinking!

I took my time getting my things together after practice. I even deliberately sat there putting my racket in its cover right next to where Hal had left his stuff, but he walked off with the other guys, without so much as a backward glance in my direction. Obviously he didn't want to give himself away in front of the other guys. I just wished I could be sure. If only he'd given me some little hint—a secret smile or a wink. But now I still didn't know.

Chapter

9

I was very nervous as my dad drove me over to Scottsdale High for the preseason invitational the next morning. The coach had called us all together after practice on Friday night and told us not to worry. This tournament was just for fun and for match readiness. It didn't count. He also warned us that we'd be meeting some top private schools we wouldn't have to face in regular-season play. "So just go out there and have fun," he said.

That was easy for him to say. I was the only girl in a guys' tournament, facing the top players in the state, and he wanted me to have fun. I might have boasted that I'd gone to the same tennis camp as Andre Agassi, but that didn't mean I'd ever had to play him! I had a horrible feeling I'd get creamed—no, worse than creamed, totally humiliated.

There were millions of tennis players hanging around at the Scottsdale courts, all of them guys, looking tall, strong, tanned, and muscled. Were these freshmen? Give me a break. Was Alta Mesa the only school in the world where the freshman guys' team made me feel like Snow White with her seven dwarves? I felt myself starting to panic. If only I could have seen one other girl, I'd have felt better. I just prayed that they'd opened the girls' locker rooms. Otherwise I'd be in big trouble before the end of the day.

I was glad the coach had given us all Alta Mesa T-shirts. At least that took away the decision about what to wear and helped me blend in. I had one embarrassing moment as I saw my teammates and started to cross the court to get to them. An official put out his hand to stop me. "Spectators to the right, little lady," he said.

"I'm a player," I told him sweetly.

"Then you've come to the wrong place," he said, also sweetly. "This is the boys' tournament. The girls are over at Hidden Valley."

"Not this girl," I said. "I'm on the boys' team at Alta Mesa." Then I swept past him in triumph. At least now I felt fighting mad and ready to take on anyone.

Hal and Marshall were standing together, talking nervously as I walked up.

"Do you see who's playing here?" Marshall whispered as I joined them. "The team from Sandhurst. I know it's only their freshman squad, but they're all state-ranked players. We are going to look so bad."

"Who did Don pick to be our fourth singles player?" I asked, looking around.

"David," Marshall said, also looking around to see if either the coach or David was within earshot.

"David?" I said in alarm. "You mean the little guy who swings and misses completely half the time?"

"He's got a good hard shot when he doesn't miss," Hal said, and I noticed that he had a nice twinkle in his eye when he smiled.

"He's the best we've got right now," Marshall said. "I wish Danny hadn't quit."

"He didn't quit," I said. "He was kicked off the team."

"Uh, right," Marshall said, looking embarrassed. "But we could sure use him now. It's like giving away three matches."

"So where is David?" Hal demanded. "He better hurry up and get here or we'll miss our warm-up time."

I looked around. There, crossing the crowded court and heading in our direction, was Danny. I almost yelled out loud, but I swallowed it at the last second. I didn't want him to know I was pleased to see him.

He was dressed for tennis and he had his racket in his hand. My heart gave a tremendous lurch. He looked as handsome as ever with his mop of dark hair and that cocky walk with the slight swagger to it. It was the same old confident Danny.

It occurred to me that maybe he was ready to forgive and forget. I found myself wondering what I'd do if he acted like he wanted to start over. Did I want him back after the way he treated me? After all, he'd made me feel pretty bad. He hadn't thought about my feelings at all. If I were a strong woman, I should never forgive behavior like that. But I couldn't help it. If he gave me that special, wonderful smile, I'd smile right back at him.

"Danny!" Marshall yelled joyously. "It's good to see you, old buddy." He held out his hand and Danny slapped it. "Are you going to be our fourth?"

"Looks like it," Danny said. "How you doing, Hal, buddy? Good to see ya." Then he looked at me, his face expressionless. "Hi," he said.

"Hi," I returned.

"I hear you're getting pretty good," Danny ventured.

"We'll see today."

We stood there, facing each other like two boxers who have just stepped into the ring.

113

"Personally I think we're all going to get our butts kicked today," Hal said, hastily stepping between us. "But if anyone has a chance of winning, I'd say it was Justine."

I beamed at him. What a sweet guy. What a nice thing to say. I studied him from beneath my bangs as I rummaged in my sports bag. Definitely the type of boy to send secret messages on big, red hearts. But did I want a new boyfriend? Was I ready yet? Then I thought how jealous Danny would be if he saw me with Hal. Two weeks on the team and she starts dating the only sophomore! This definitely had possibilities. After all, I didn't have to fall in love with him, did I?

"So . . . uh . . . how come you're back on the team, Danny?" Marshall asked. "Did the coach ask you to come back?"

"You know it," Danny said. "He didn't exactly crawl or kiss my feet, but pretty close to it. I knew he would, of course." He shot me a triumphant look. "He pointed out that you guys didn't stand a chance without me, and I decided it was fine. After all, whatever happened with me and Justine was all over anyway. So it's fine with me if she goes or stays, as long as she wins matches for us."

He stared at me, his eyes challenging. I returned his stare. I knew he was exaggerating about the coach. Don would never beg a player to come back. Danny was just trying to psych me out. Well, he wasn't going to! I'd had years of practice at hiding the way I really felt. All those schools where I was desperately unhappy and the other girls shut me out of their cliques. All those times my father didn't show up for visiting day. Oh yes, I was great at not letting anyone know what I was feeling inside. And today I was making a special effort. It was really, really important for me to do well at this tournament. If I thought about Danny, I wouldn't play my best. So I made a great mental effort and shut him from my mind.

Don appeared, trying to look cheerful and relaxed. "I've got your schedules here, guys. Justine, I'm afraid I've let you in for a hard time. I put you as our number one, and you're going to come up against some pretty experienced players. But don't worry about it. It's all good experience. You might psych them out when they find they're playing against a girl."

Fat chance of that, I thought. I took my schedule from him. We had a brief warm-up. I thought Danny might be a little rusty, since he hadn't worked out with us, but he was good.

"I took some lessons with the pro at my dad's country club," I heard him say to Marshall. "I didn't want to look like a total lame-o if I came back."

I started to relax. This was going to work out okay

after all. I really could handle it. The bell sounded for the end of warm-up, and I picked up my sports bag to head to court ten.

"So, Justine," Danny said as we left the court together, "I hear you're going to the dance on Friday."

I didn't say that I'd seen him hovering around while I bought my ticket. "That's right." I didn't even look up.

"So who you going with?"

"It's not formal," I said. "You don't need a partner."

"Oh," he said, and I could see the relieved grin. It's okay, he was thinking. She hasn't managed to find anyone else.

"There is someone I might go with. I haven't decided yet," I said. "I got a really sweet Valentine's card yesterday."

"Is that a fact?" he said, and then the cocky grin returned. "That's funny, because I have this new girl who's got the hots for me. So I might see you there, at the dance."

"Sure," I said. "Why not. See you around, Danny. I have a tennis game to win."

I was so cool, I was really impressed with myself. *Justine, the Ice Princess,* I thought. Wait until I told Roni and the others about it tonight. They'd be proud of me.

Then it occurred to me that each of these little encounters was driving Danny and me further and further

116

apart, until there would be no hope of our ever getting together again. Even if he had acted like a total jerk, I'd still had the best time of my life with him. He'd made me feel special once, and I couldn't forget that, however hard I tried.

I walked out onto court ten. A big, chubby boy was already standing across the net. He looked very surprised to see me. "Hi," he said, "looking for someone?"

"Yes," I said, consulting my schedule. "I'm looking for the player from Glendale."

"That's me. Tom Wilkins."

"Great. Then I'm in the right place," I said. "I'm Justine Craft from Alta Mesa. You get to play me."

He looked astonished, then a big grin spread across his face. "You're their number one?"

I shrugged.

"What's the matter, don't they have any guys at that school?" he asked.

I was very tempted to say that our best guys were currently away preparing for Wimbledon. I was also tempted to say, "None as good as me." But the new, improved, humble Justine said nothing.

I saw him shaking with amusement as he picked up some balls. He certainly was a real tub of lard. His whole body shook and quivered. I bet he couldn't run worth diddly.

The umpire called us over and tossed a coin. "One set, no adds," he said. Tom Wilkins won. As he walked back to serve, he was still grinning.

The first serve was hard, but it was also out. The second was weak, and as I came in to net the ball came flying straight at my middle. I couldn't do anything with it, except dodge out of the way.

"Sorry," he said, still grinning.

Okay, if that's how you want it, I thought. He so clearly thought it would be a piece of cake to play against me. He was hitting very hard. I think he hoped he'd scare me in the first game and I'd run away crying.

He won the first game, but only because he got a couple of lucky serves in. Then it was my turn. My serve clearly surprised him. When I hit a short one and he came in to net, I sent a ball straight at his middle. I could hear him grunt "Oof" as it hit him.

"Sorry," I said sweetly.

That made him mad. And as we continued playing, he got madder and madder. The best moment came when he was standing way back and I put a drop shot just over the net. I had been right. He couldn't run. He came waddling up too late to reach it, and I heard a laugh from the spectators. I hadn't realized anybody was watching us. I was shocked to see people lined up behind the wire.

"Good shot," someone called.

After that it was easy. I wound up winning six-two. Tom didn't even wait around to shake hands. When I found my teammates again, it turned out that I was the only one who had won a match.

"Those guys are tough," Danny was saying. He looked up as I arrived. "So, how did it go, Justine?"

"I won, six-two," I said calmly.

They were clearly impressed. But I knew it was probably too good to last. My first glance at my next opponent told me that he wasn't going to collapse at the thought of playing a girl. He nodded seriously to me as I came onto the court and shook hands. "Sandhurst" was embroidered on his shirt and matching shorts. His first serve told me that we were now in another league altogether. He was very, very good.

I found that I was playing my hardest against him, making shots I didn't even know I could. But whatever I did, he had an answer for it. He wound up beating me six-love. After the game I was drenched in sweat and totally exhausted. As I came to net to shake his hand, I was surprised to hear applause. A large crowd had been watching us.

"Good game," someone yelled. Must have been someone from Sandhurst. It hadn't been a good game for me. I'd looked totally stupid.

My opponent shook hands with me. "Nice game," he said.

"Yeah, right," I said, managing a smile. "You creamed me."

"You were tougher than I thought you'd be," he said. "It's not exactly fair to have you play in a guys' tournament."

He was being nice to me, and I hated it. He was just rubbing in kindly that girls didn't belong in guys' sports. At that moment, I agreed with him. I just wanted to get out of there, away from all those gawking spectators. I knew they were all feeling sorry for me.

"Justine!" Danny's voice made me look up with a start. "So, how did you do?"

"He beat me, six-love," I said flatly.

"Oh, that's too bad," Danny said. I thought I caught just the hint of a smirk. That did it.

"I bet I just made your day, right?" I yelled. "This proves your point, Danny. This shows that you're right and I'm wrong. The moment I met a good player, I looked like a total fool. I bet you'll laugh yourself silly over this, but you better just stay away from me!"

I swept past him, pushed my way out of the court, and kept on going. I'd go home now. I wouldn't stay around to finish this tournament.

I heard footsteps hurrying behind me, but I didn't turn around. Even if Danny wanted to apologize now, I wasn't going to listen. "Excuse me," an unfamiliar voice called.

I stopped and looked back. It wasn't Danny. It was a strange man.

"Hi, I'm Coach Hauser, from Sandhurst School," he said. He was a big, older man who looked like a tennis player, very lean and tanned. "I watched you play Tim just now."

I nodded. "He was too good for me."

"You gave him a good game."

"He beat me six-love," I pointed out.

"You made him fight for every point. That woke him up in a hurry, I can tell you," Coach Hauser said. "It was the best thing that could have happened to him. He's been getting lazy. He was way too cocky coming into this season. Ever since he got his current national ranking, all he can think about is getting a scholarship and turning pro."

"H-he's nationally ranked?" I stammered.

"You didn't know? He was the best fourteen and under in Arizona. Now that he's turned fifteen he's dropped a little, but not much."

"Oh," I said. Maybe I had won some points after all.

Coach Hauser smiled. "Who coaches you?"

"I'm on the team at Alta Mesa."

"Yes, I can see that. I mean which pro do you work with?"

"I don't. I used to take lessons when I went to

Sagebrush, and I've been to a couple of camps . . ."

He nodded. "Sagebrush has a good program. That's why you've got such nice ground strokes." He was looking at me very intently now. "I could really use you on my girls' team," he said.

"Excuse me?" I didn't think I'd heard right.

"My frosh-soph girls' team is weak this year, by our standards," he said. "You probably know we have the best tennis program in the state. I could really use you. I could turn you into a fine player. All the best colleges recruit from us. You'd have it made."

"But I've just started at Alta Mesa," I said. "I can't switch schools in midyear."

"Sure you can," he said, smiling easily now. "If we move you across before the season officially starts, it will be legal to have you play for us. We have a good academic program, too. You're wasted where you are. You'll never be able to be a real star in a guys' league. So what do you say?"

"I don't know what to say," I said.

"Then think it over," Coach Hauser said. "Talk to your parents. I'm sure they'd see the advantages of going to a school like Sandhurst, especially since you've been to Sagebrush. Tell you what—why don't you come on a tour on Monday. Bring your folks. I'll introduce you to the principal and you can meet the kids, and then we can see about getting the transfer in motion."

I was in a daze as I made my way back to my team.

"How did you do, Justine?" Marshall asked me.

"What? Oh, I lost," I said.

"Join the club," Hal said. "We're getting our butts kicked real bad. Frankly I don't think that Alta Mesa is what you'd call a good tennis school. Maybe we should all transfer to Sandhurst if we really want to play."

He said it with a grin. I was the only one who wasn't laughing.

I might just do that, I thought. *There's nothing for me here anymore.*

Chapter

10

"Justine?"

I looked up from the garden swing where I was curled up with a large bowl of cookies-and-cream ice cream—my favorite tranquilizer. My mind had been miles away, playing tennis at Sandhurst and being recruited by Stanford before turning pro. I was just playing at my first Wimbledon when the loud voice cut through my daydream.

"What?"

Christine, my stepmother, was standing in front of me, looking like a ship in full sail.

"You weren't listening to a word I was saying, were you?"

"Sorry," I muttered. Usually I made an effort to be

polite to her these days, and she usually tried to be nice to me. But the way she was talking now reminded me of the way things had been at the beginning.

"What did you say?" I asked coldly.

"I reminded you that your friends will be arriving pretty soon and your room still looks like a disaster area."

"Oh," I said. "It's okay. They won't mind. They know me by now."

I went back to shoveling ice cream into my mouth.

"But that's just not right, Justine," Christine said in that annoyingly patient way adults have. "You can't expect your friends to sleep on a floor piled high with clothes."

"It's not piled high with clothes," I muttered. "I just couldn't decide which pair of shorts to wear this morning. I happen to have a lot of shorts."

"You should want to do something special for your friends," Christine said. "They've been very good for you this year. They've helped you get into the mainstream at Alta Mesa very quickly."

A big gulping sob unexpectedly shook my whole body, making me cough as a spoonful of ice cream went down the wrong way. Going to Sandhurst would mean leaving the best friends I'd ever had in my life. I hadn't even thought about that. All I'd thought about was becoming a tennis star and getting as far away from Danny as I could.

Christine slid beside me onto the swing, making it rock violently. She's no lightweight anymore. She patted my back until I'd finished coughing.

"Is something the matter, Justine?" she asked, more gently now. "You look like you've got something on your mind. Are you still feeling bad about losing today?"

I shook my head.

"You're not in any kind of trouble, are you?"

"No, nothing like that," I said. "It's just that . . ." I hesitated. Did I want to tell my stepmother about this? Then I remembered that she'd have to know in the end. The coach had invited my parents on the tour of Sandhurst, too. And it was obvious that they'd have to be in on the final decision, right? "It's just that the coach at Sandhurst School saw me play today and he wants me to transfer there, to play for him."

She was definitely impressed. "Justine, how flattering for you. But you wouldn't want to go, would you? I mean, correct me if I'm wrong, but isn't Sandhurst another Sagebrush, a school for spoiled rich kids? Wasn't that exactly what we were trying to get you away from?"

"But it's the best tennis school in Arizona," I said. "I might be a champion someday."

"Is that what you want?"

126

I shrugged. "Sounds good to me," I said. "Playing tennis all over the world, million-dollar endorsements . . ."

"I wonder how many of those girls are really happy, though," Christine said thoughtfully. "It's a tough life. And lonely too, I imagine."

"That's okay," I said. "I'm used to being lonely."

"I don't know what your father will think about this," Christine said. "It needs talking about. He was the one who wanted you to go to a regular public school and stop acting like a spoiled brat."

"I was not a spoiled brat," I snapped. Then I shrugged. "Okay, so maybe just a little. And I know what Daddy will say. As soon as he hears that I'll get the top tennis coaching in the state, he'll be all for it. He'll be able to brag about me to all his friends at the club."

Christine laughed and covered my hand with hers. "You're right. That's exactly what he'd do. 'My daughter the tennis star!' I can just hear him. Then he'll bore them with a blow-by-blow description of your latest match."

We were both laughing now.

Then Christine sighed. "Oh, dear. What a difficult decision, Justine. There's more to this than just tennis. There's the whole question of academics and the kind of kids you'd be mixing with."

"I didn't say I definitely did want to go," I told her.

"I'm only thinking about it. The coach wants us to take a tour so that we can see the school for ourselves and I can meet the team members."

"All right," Christine said. "We can certainly do that. Your dad's on that business trip until Wednesday. Would you like me to go with you?"

"Okay."

"And Justine," she said. "I don't think we'll mention this to your father until you've had a chance to see the school. We don't want him making this decision for you. You know he'll go overboard when he sees all those tennis courts."

We looked at each other and grinned like conspirators. It was really different talking to her instead of my father. In my past life, before he met Christine, I'd tell him something, and then he'd decide what I was going to do. Christine made me feel that it was my decision, too. I liked that. I was only just beginning to realize that having a mother had definite advantages.

"And now you'd better get that room cleaned up," she said. "I'd come and give you a hand, only I don't think I'll ever be able to get out of this seat again. I knew it was a mistake the moment I sat here."

I looked at her, sprawled awkwardly among the pillows. Then I took both her hands and yanked her to her feet.

By the time the first of my friends arrived at seven-thirty, my room looked like a designer showcase. All the white lace pillows were in place on my canopy bed. All my stuffed animals were sitting on the shelf. All my books were on the bookcase. What's more, there was a big jug of fresh lemonade in the fridge and a bake-it-yourself pizza waiting to go in the oven. There was popcorn in the air popper and Oreo cookies waiting to be dunked into milk. We were all set for a sleepover.

I paced around the unfamiliarly clean room and sat in my white wicker rocking chair, rocking myself as I stared out of the window. An evening breeze had sprung up, and the palm trees were rustling and swaying in a crazy dance. I tried to be excited about my friends coming in a few minutes, but my brain was still going a mile a minute. Should I tell them about Sandhurst? Wouldn't I want their input on something as big as that? But I knew what they'd say. They'd just think I was being snobby old Justine again, rushing back to my former life at the first sign of stress.

"But I'm not running away, I'm running toward," I told myself. "I only want to see how far I can go with my talent."

When I put it like that, it sounded pretty good. That

was definitely how I'd put it to everyone if and when I finally decided I wanted to transfer. Even Danny would appreciate that. I sighed as I thought about Danny. It seemed impossible that only a couple of weeks ago we had been an item, holding hands around school, kidding around in the cafeteria.

School and tennis and Danny and my friends raced around my head. It was too much to worry about. There were too many big decisions to make. I hated it! Teenage years weren't supposed to be like this. They were supposed to be fun and carefree, full of harmless activities like the sleepover that was about to happen. At least when my friends got here I'd have my mind taken off all these worries. Just for tonight I'd forget that there was a big decision I had to make. We'd have fun, we'd be silly, I'd help them plan for the big Valentine's Day Dance, and I wouldn't mention Sandhurst to them at all!

Just when I had made that momentous decision the doorbell rang. It was Roni. She staggered up the stairs under the load of her sleeping bag and an overstuffed sports bag. I really don't understand why my friends still haven't gotten around to coordinated luggage. I couldn't go anywhere unless I matched. But I'd learned to keep quiet about things like that, because my friends got offended. Also I knew they didn't have the kind of money I was used to. If I went to Sandhurst, I bet all the girls would be coordinated, all the time!

"Hi," Roni puffed. "Boy am I tired. Do you know that the coach put me in the mile today? Do you know how long a mile is? Very long. I felt like I was running between here and L.A."

"So how did you do?"

"Not too bad, considering I'd never run it before," she said. "I came in sixth. At least I wasn't last. Of course, the other girls had somebody cheering for them. My family went to my sister's softball game, and Chris was at that nerdy thing with Walter."

"I can't believe Chris still actually hangs around with him by choice." I wrinkled my nose in disgust.

"I know," she said. "Am I making a terrible mistake, Justine?"

"Yes!" I exclaimed. "I really think we should get you back with Drew as quickly as possible."

"You think so?"

"I know so. Drew is a real status date. Chris is . . . well . . . just the opposite. Has Drew said anything more about the dance to you?"

"Sort of," Roni said. "He passed me on the way back from baseball last night. He was with a group of guys, the way he always is, and he said, 'So, did you get your dance ticket yet? You better be there.'"

"What does that mean?" I demanded. "Why can't he just come out and ask you if he wants you to go with him? Guys are so annoying."

"But I can't go with Drew now, can I?" Roni snapped. "I already said yes to Chris."

"You're still in love with Drew. Admit it."

Roni sighed hopelessly. "I do still miss him, Justine. He was so wonderful. But I also have to be reasonable and admit he was more crush than boyfriend. I can't go through life worshiping a guy just because he's gorgeous and fun, can I?"

"Why not? It sounds better than a date with a nerd," I said.

"I know," she said, "but Chris is so sweet, and he's fun to be around too, when he's on his own. Remember that we're planning to be in the spring play together? But I can't help having terrible second thoughts about the dance on Friday."

The doorbell rang again.

This time it was Karen.

"Hi," she said as she stomped upstairs. "Just don't talk to me for the next hour. I'm in a bad mood."

"What happened?" Roni and I asked in unison. Karen just wasn't the grouchy type. I could see Roni or Ginger stomping up the stairs and flinging down her sleeping bag. I could even see me doing it.

But not Karen.

"Bad day all around, I guess," Karen said. "First I have to put up with a lecture from my parents about going to this track meet. I usually have a violin lesson on Saturday mornings, and I changed it without asking my parents. When they saw me leaving the house without my violin, they had a fit. You'd have thought that joining the track team was the same as dancing in a strip joint."

"You should have told them it was a required freshman activity. That always worked before."

"I didn't get a chance. Anything that takes me away from my violin just has to be bad in their eyes."

She lay back on my bed with a sigh. Roni and I exchanged glances. "And then there was James," she said.

"James? What did he do?"

She sat up again. "You know what a jerk he's being about the Valentine's Day Dance?" she demanded. "He really doesn't want to go, so he pretends like he's making this huge sacrifice for my sake, just showing up there for ten minutes. And now I find out that he wants to wear his red suspenders and his Doctor Seuss hat."

Roni and I couldn't help it. We looked at each other and started giggling. And the harder we tried to stop, the more we giggled.

133

Karen glared at us. "It's not funny, you guys," she said. "I mean, can you see me dancing with someone who looks like the Cat in the Hat when everyone else is semiformal? I'll die of embarrassment, and I'm sure that's what he's counting on. He thinks that I'll lose my cool and say we won't go."

"Boy, what a jerk," I said.

"Who'd have thought that James would turn out to be such a pain, too," Roni said. "First Danny, then Chris, and now James."

"What has Chris done?" Karen asked.

"Nothing really terrible, I suppose," Roni said. "But he wouldn't come cheer for my track meet today because he'd rather be with Walter, and he also wouldn't promise me that he'd keep away from the nerds at the dance. He says they're his friends and he owes them enough to be polite to them. How can I go to a dance, knowing I'll be surrounded by nerds all night?"

"You'll be as embarrassed as I will," Karen agreed. "Chris might even offer to let Ronald or Owen dance with you."

"Or Walter!" Roni sighed. "I'm doomed, guys. I don't even think I want to go now."

"And we were all looking forward to the dance so much," I said. "We all thought it would be the most romantic evening of the year."

At that moment Ginger came flying up the stairs, her face red with anger.

"Uggh, boys!" she yelled. "I never want to see another boy again as long as I live!"

Chapter 11

We all stared at Ginger as she flung down her bag next to Karen's and stomped across the room.

"Can we go for a swim?" she asked. "I want to disappear under the water and just lie there until I can calm down again."

"You had a fight with Ben?" Roni ventured.

"Major fight," Ginger said. "And I thought he was such a great guy, too. Now I find out what he's really like. A total sexist creep like the rest of them."

"Ginger, what happened?" Karen asked, going over to her and putting a friendly hand on her shoulder.

"It was so dumb," Ginger said, blinking back a tear. "All about dumb baseball."

Karen sat her down, and I handed her my box of tissues and the dish of M&Ms. "Ben was mad this morning because I wasn't going to cheer for him at his baseball game," she said.

"But you had a track meet!" Roni exclaimed indignantly.

"I know," Ginger said. "I told him. And you know what he said? He said, 'Well, it's only a practice meet and it's only track.'"

"Only track?" I shrieked. "That boy needs a kick."

"I can't believe it," Karen exclaimed. "He really wanted you to give up your own chance to compete just to cheer for him?"

"He didn't exactly say that," Ginger said, "but that was what he meant."

"Sexist pig," I muttered. Shades of Danny all over again. What was wrong with these guys?

"And then . . ." Ginger went on.

"There's more?"

She nodded. "It gets worse. The baseball team has an away game on Friday after school, and Ben doesn't think they'll get back until after eight."

"So you'll be really late to the dance," Roni commented.

"Worse than that," Ginger said. "Ben thought he was being all calm and reasonable, telling me how he was sure I understood how important baseball is to him, and then he said, 'So would you really mind too much if we didn't go to the dance, because I'm going to be pretty pooped . . . and it's not like it's the junior prom or anything.'"

"But he must have known how excited you were about it!" I cried.

She nodded and took one of the tissues Karen was holding out to her. "I reminded him I'd already bought the tickets, and you know what he said? 'Don't worry, I'll pay you back for them.' Pay me back? As if that was what mattered!" She jumped up and started pacing the room like a caged animal. "It's like I don't really matter as a person at all."

"I know just how you feel, Ginger," I said. I got up and started pacing with her. "It's like déjà vu all over again."

"Déjà vu *is* all over again, Justine," Karen said patiently.

Ginger and Roni laughed, but I went right on. "Danny was totally cool until he saw me as competition. Then he freaked out. It seems like guys just can't handle girls being jocks, too."

"They can't handle girls having a life of their own, period, if you ask me," Karen said, joining in the pacing. "They want us to admire them and tell them they're wonderful. That's all we're supposed to do. James has been making all these little jokes about high jumping being a waste of time, and he was upset because I wouldn't come to the computer show with him. He pouted, just like a baby, and he said, 'But you always come to my computer things with me! Who will I have to explain things to?'"

"That's just what Ben said," Ginger exclaimed, smiling now. "He said, 'But you always come cheer for me. I know I'll screw up if you're not there.'"

"Just like little kids!" Roni said. "Like it's your fault if they screw up."

"That's exactly what Danny did when we were playing tennis. He served a fault and then glared at me."

"Boy, what a bunch of wimps," Roni growled. "Selfish, immature . . ."

"Sexist . . ."

"Pathetic . . ."

"Hold on, guys," I wailed. "I can't think of any more good adjectives!"

"We deserve better than this," Ginger said. "We deserve guys who are proud of us and support us whatever we do."

"Right on," Roni yelled, making a fist. "And who care about our feelings enough to know that we freak out when surrounded by nerds."

"And don't feel threatened by us if we're better at a sport than they are," I added.

"And want us to be happy," Karen said with a sigh. "Do you think that any boys like that really exist?"

139

"Maybe when they grow up," Roni said dubiously, "but not at fourteen or fifteen."

"Or sixteen," Ginger added. "Ben's already sixteen."

She slumped back onto my bed. We joined her, lying back among my pillows. "I always dreamed of my first boyfriend," Karen said. "I thought that, once I had a boyfriend, everything would be wonderful and he'd bring me flowers and life would be really romantic. Instead of that he wants me to watch him program animated monsters into computers!"

"And hang out with nerds for him!"

"And watch him play baseball and football and every other sort of ball," Ginger yelled.

I sat up, scattering pillows over my friends' faces. "You know what I think?" I demanded. "I think we'd all be better off without boys. I mean, look at us. We have a great friendship. We hardly ever fight. We care about each other. I think boys our age have a lot of growing up to do, while we're already mature and sophisticated women." I waved my arms a little too dramatically, sending a cascade of stuffed animals down onto my friends.

"Justine!" Roni yelled as a large dinosaur landed on her head.

"Well, I think Justine is right," Karen said, thoughtfully stroking a soft white unicorn. "Those boys have got

140

a lot of growing up to do. And I think it's up to us to teach them a lesson. They've got to find out that they have to treat girls with respect at all times, or they're going to be lonely old men some day."

"How do we tell them that?" Roni asked. "You know boys hate hearing lectures from girls. They don't even take us seriously."

"I think we should try shock therapy," Ginger said suddenly.

"You mean hit Danny on the head with my tennis racket and yell at him while he's lying unconscious?" I asked.

"I mean show them that we don't need them to take us to the dance," Ginger said slowly.

We looked at each other, trying to digest this.

"Where would we find other dates now, even if we wanted to?" Karen asked worriedly. "All the good boys are already taken."

"We'll go without dates," Ginger said. "We'll go stag, just like all the macho guys do, so we can check out the guys when we get there. We'll hang out together. We'll dance just on our own, in a group. We'll show those guys that we can have a good time at a dance without a dumb boy."

"You really think we can do that?" Roni asked nervously.

"Sure. Guys go stag all the time. And if our boy-friends—correction, former boyfriends—come to the dance, it will send them a message that we don't need them around to have fun."

"That's a great idea," I said. "I like that. Four women of the nineties, powerful, confident . . . we need to go shopping tomorrow. I have to get some powerful clothes."

"Wait a minute," Roni interrupted. She turned to Ginger. "Did you say *former* boyfriends?"

Ginger nodded.

"You're going to break up with Ben?"

"Until he learns his lesson," Ginger said. "He's going to see how well I can survive without him, and then he's going to wake up."

"That's a great idea," Karen said. "James was totally beginning to take me for granted. I bet it would wake him up too if I told him he shouldn't bother coming to the dance. I'd be quite happy going with my girl-friends."

"And I could let Chris know that it was either the nerds or me," Roni said with a big satisfied smile. "And Justine could show that creep Danny how easy it was to get over him."

"I love it!" I yelled. "Woman power! We're free! We're empowered—there's nothing we can't do!"

"We should make banners or something," Karen said.

"We can start a whole movement!" Ginger agreed.

142

"We'll get all the girls in the freshman class to give up dating until the boys treat us right!"

"It will spread throughout the world! We'll be famous!" Roni shrieked. "Women everywhere will thank us. They'll ask us to make speeches to Congress."

"So how do we start?" Karen asked, nervously licking her lips. She always was the practical one.

"Wait, I've got a great idea!" I jumped up and ran to my closet. I began throwing down piles of T-shirts from the shelf.

"What are you doing, Justine?" Karen asked.

"I've got fabric markers somewhere," I said, "and I'm sure I've got at least four plain T-shirts. We can make our statements and then wear them to school. People will see them and ask us what they stand for and we can spread the word."

"Great idea!" Ginger said. "How lucky that the Valentine's Dance is coming up. We'll get all the girls to go without their dates. We'll show those stupid guys that girls don't need them around for a good time."

My friends started scrabbling on the floor among the T-shirts. "Where are the markers, Justine? I can't wait to get started."

"I've never seen so many T-shirts," Roni exclaimed. "You could open a store."

"One can never have too many T-shirts," I said

haughtily. "They're a basic fashion necessity. Not the dime-store kind, of course—you'll find that all mine have designer labels, except for the Mickey Mouse one . . . hey, stop laughing!"

We found the markers and worked feverishly for the next hour. We agreed on a sign for the front of the shirts. It was a circle with a slash through it and it said NO MORE BOYS. On the back we wrote things like WOMAN POWER. FREE TO BE ME. DRESSED FOR SUCCESS. TRACK STAR. I wrote TENNIS PRO. It felt good.

Then we put them on and admired ourselves in my closet door mirror.

"This will wake them up in a hurry," Roni said. "I can't wait to see their faces. Chris will be bewildered. Ben will freak out."

"So will James."

"So will Danny."

We grinned at each other delightedly.

"Now we have to seriously plan our strategy," Ginger said. "We don't have much time to get the message to all the freshman girls before the dance. We have speeches to write . . ."

"Banners," Karen said. "We need lots of banners."

"We'll have to find out about permission to hold protest marches."

"TV coverage," I said. "We should get the media

144

involved. No more fooling around. We need to get serious here. We have to work day and night."

There was a tap on my door.

"Sorry to interrupt," Christine said. "I just wanted you to know that the pizza is in the oven and almost ready."

"Pizza!" my friends all yelled at the same time. They fought each other to charge down the stairs. Christine looked at my room with T-shirts all over my floor and the furniture, the paper with practice drawings on it, and the open markers.

"Holy cow," she exclaimed.

"It's okay, Christine. We're just women of the nineties expressing our individuality."

When we got to school on Monday morning we saw right away that Valentine fever was already taking hold. Even the girls' bathrooms had red hearts in them. There were notices all over the walls about the last day to sign up for candygrams, the right place to order red roses, and even where to hire a limo. We met at the front entrance, took off our jackets so that our shirts were visible, and walked down the hall. Nobody said a word. Nobody even noticed. Everyone we passed was in the middle of a conversation about the dance:

"Did you find a dress you liked?"

"I made a nail appointment right after school on Friday."

"I wish I knew whether to get my hair cut or not. What do you think?"

Ginger glared at us. "Everyone in the world has been zapped into a mushy pink twilight zone," she said. "It's all up to us now. We have to make them see that they're throwing their lives away before it's too late."

"How do we do that?" Karen asked nervously. "Stand in the middle of the hall and yell slogans until we get trampled to death?"

"We'll have a lunch-hour meeting," Ginger said. "We'll put up our own notices. We'll spread the word in all our classes and we'll meet under our tree. Come on, let's get busy. Who's got paper and markers? Not you, Justine, your printing is terrible. No one will be able to read it."

"Fine," I said, tossing my hair as I turned away. I knew Ginger was always blunt, but it still hurt when she talked to me like that. It made me feel that I wasn't really one of the group.

"Here, Justine," Roni said, handing me a piece of paper. "You get to go put them up on all the walls."

"Gee, thanks a lot. What am I—chief slave?"

"We're writing our hands off here, Justine. Someone has to get them on the walls before school or it will be

146

too late," Karen said, not looking up from the paper she was printing on in neat red and green letters.

Thanks to my speed and efficiency, we managed to get quite a few notices up on the walls. The problem was that there were already so many notices about the dance that there wasn't much space.

I wasn't sure that anyone would read our signs.

When we reached our classroom, our shirts got noticed for the first time.

"What's that supposed to mean?" one of the guys demanded, pointing to our symbol with the line through it.

"It means we've had enough of being taken for granted by immature guys who want us to share their lives but aren't prepared to share ours," Ginger said. "Our mission is to wake up all the freshman girls before it's too late."

"We're going to get all the girls in the school to join us and give up dating," Roni cut in.

"You want the girls to do what?" cried a girl.

"Are you crazy?" a girl in the back shrieked. "It's right before Valentine's Day, and I, for one, am hoping for a large box of chocolate."

"I bought a new dress for the dance. I'm not taking it back now," another girl chimed in.

"You can still go to the dance, just not with your date," Ginger explained.

"What for? That's no fun. I only go for the slow dances."

"I guess you girls are just mad that you couldn't find dates, right?" one of the guys shouted triumphantly. Then all the rest of them started in with dumb comments. It was clear that our message hadn't been an immediate success.

"All new ideas have to start slowly," Roni said as we took our seats to laughter and rude remarks. "At least we've made our point of view known. We just have to wait for the word to get around."

"Give them time to think about it," Karen agreed. "By lunchtime they'll have decided that we're right. You'll see."

They all seemed pretty confident that we were doing the right thing. It was becoming clearer by the minute that every other girl in this school was looking forward to the dance and the red roses and everything else that Valentine's Day stood for, and they weren't about to be cheated out of it by us.

The news spread all right, just like Ginger said it would. Now we got jeers in the hallways between classes from kids we didn't even know.

Worst of all, Danny came past with his friends. "Sore loser, huh, Justine?" he said, grinning. "You couldn't have the cutest guy in the class, so now you want to stop everyone else from having fun."

"On the contrary, I want them to see that it's more fun not wasting their lives on some jerk who doesn't appreciate them," I said. "We want them to see that there's more to life than dating." I was wonderfully calm. I was proud of myself.

"So what about this cool dude who you were planning to go to the dance with instead of me?" Danny asked with a smirk. "You just made him up, right? I knew there wasn't really anyone."

My secret admirer! In my new feminist excitement I'd forgotten all about him. He wanted to meet me at the dance. Was I really going to tell him to get lost just to be true to my new principles? Even if he turned out to be gorgeous? Even if he was Hal? This needed a lot of thinking about.

At lunchtime we stood by our tree, and not a single girl showed up.

"Okay," Ginger said, taking a deep breath. "We have to realize that this may take a little time. We've sprung it on them too suddenly."

"And at a bad psychological moment," Karen finished for her. "They're all looking forward to the dance. Valentine's Day represents what's best about dating. No girl is going to turn down the chance for romance."

"I guess you're right," Ginger agreed. She gave a big

sigh. "So it looks like it's only us. But we won't be moved, right?"

"Right," Roni said. "If we want to change the way guys treat us, we have to stand firm and stand together."

"We'll be pioneers," Ginger agreed. "Women of the future will thank us."

I just wished I could share their optimism. I had the feeling we'd be the only four wallflowers at the dance, while everyone else was having a good time. My friends were subdued and a little down as we went back for afternoon classes. I had other things on my mind—my secret admirer, whoever he was.

And my upcoming tour of Sandhurst.

Chapter 12

Christine was coming to pick me up at two-thirty. She was going to call and get permission for me to miss last period, so that we could get to Sandhurst before school was out for the day. I still hadn't mentioned it to my friends, mainly because I knew how they'd react. They would never understand that I might want to go to a school like that. But then, what did they know? They'd never had the chance to go to a good private school. I had, and the thought of one with twelve tennis courts and a great coach was sounding better and better.

I told my friends that I had a dentist's appointment before last period. Then I ran into the bathroom to change. I wasn't about to tour an exclusive school in a homemade T-shirt that read "No More Boys." I was dedicated, but not stupid. I put on clothes that were more suitable for Sandhurst—a white lacy blouse, a short red plaid kilt, and a black velvet vest. I'd show them I knew what preppy meant.

Sandhurst was impressive, right from our first glimpse of it, up a long, landscaped driveway, bordered by stately palm trees. It was a modern building—all steel and glass—but it had been designed to fit into the red rock around it so that it looked more like a private home than a school.

Coach Hauser was in the cool marble entranceway, waiting for us. He jumped up and shook our hands. Then he took us on a tour of the school. Even Christine was impressed, I could tell. The most up-to-date lab facilities, a ceramics workshop in the art complex, a fantastic aquatic center with a separate diving pool, a fully equipped stage in the auditorium—there was nothing money hadn't provided here. We peeked into a classroom where a small group of kids was sitting around a teacher, discussing things informally. "There's only girls in this class," I exclaimed.

"Ah, that must be math, then," the coach said. "They've discovered that girls learn math and science better when they don't feel threatened by boys. So this school offers the opportunity for single-sex classes. Our girls score really high on the math SAT, so it must work."

I gazed at the girls, already envying them. They were all dressed like me—not in plaid skirts, but with the same kind of designer flair. I nodded in appreciation.

"Our biggest classes have only about sixteen kids," Coach Hauser said. "We like to keep things small and informal."

We got to the gym. No red hearts here. "Aren't they having a Valentine's Dance?" I asked.

"Oh sure, but we hold all our dances at the Shadows Resort," Coach Hauser said. "They do such a nice job, and the kids here don't want to get all dressed up just to dance in a gym."

I couldn't have agreed with him more. At last we came to the tennis courts. The bell sounded, and Coach Hauser's players started to arrive. The boy who had beaten me on Saturday grinned and said hello in a friendly way. "Sure beats Alta Mesa, right?" he asked, waving at the newly surfaced courts and the clubhouse. Several girls strolled up. "Over here, ladies," Coach Hauser yelled. "I want you to meet Justine."

The girls all looked like real tennis players. They smiled at me. "Is she the one you were telling us about, Coach?" one of them asked.

The coach nodded. "She's the one. A real power server, Alissa."

"Cool." Alissa turned to me. "Coach told us he'd found someone to save our frosh squad from embarrassment this year. We sure need you, Justine."

"Don't I know you?" a second girl asked. "Weren't you in the junior golf program at Mountain Walk Country Club?"

"Yes," I told her. "I thought you looked familiar, too."

"And the coach says you went to Sagebrush," another girl said. "I was there for a year. Weren't you in Saguaro Dorm with Molly Pederson? How did you like it there?"

"It was okay," I said.

She made a face. "Sandhurst is way better. Everyone's so friendly here. There were too many cliques at Sagebrush, weren't there?"

I nodded.

"Whatever made you go to Alta Mesa?" the girl asked, wrinkling her nose as if there were a bad smell. "I mean, public schools are bad enough, but Alta Mesa doesn't even get kids from the best part of town. Don't you just feel like a fish out of water there?"

"Of course she does. That's why she's coming here, dummy," another girl said with a laugh. "Would you choose Alta Mesa over Sandhurst? Especially their tennis program—talk about embarrassing. They're a joke, aren't they, Justine?"

154

"Pretty bad," I had to agree, "but then tennis isn't their thing."

"Of course not. How many kids there belong to country clubs?"

Another girl took my arm. "Everyone is so nice here, Justine, so supportive, especially if you're on the tennis team. You get extra tutoring if you fall behind in school work, and we go to fabulous tournaments all across the country."

"We're going to a tournament in Las Vegas, right, Coach?"

Coach Hauser grinned. "We'll see about that. You have to win your regular season first."

We watched warm-ups for a little while and then we walked on. "So what do you think, Justine? Pretty impressive, huh? Not like Alta Mesa?" Coach Hauser asked me.

"Definitely not like Alta Mesa," I agreed. It was scary, but I had felt immediately at home here. It was like this was a game I'd played before. I knew the rules. I knew what to say and how to act. I'd grown up with girls like this in schools like this. I knew I'd fit in right away. And maybe I'd turn into a top tennis player.

"We'll have to discuss this with Justine's father," Christine said to the coach. "But I agree that your school is certainly very impressive. We just have to

155

make sure it's the best thing for Justine right now."

"What could be better?" Coach Hauser exclaimed. "Tell her dad if he sends her to me, I'll turn her into a tennis star."

I had visions of glory in my head as we drove home. Wait until I told Roni and Ginger and Karen about this—they'd be so impressed!

But then it suddenly struck me. If I transferred to Sandhurst, there would be no more Roni or Ginger or Karen.

On Tuesday the first decision I had to make was whether to wear my NO MORE BOYS T-shirt again. My friends insisted they were going to keep them on until their message got through. But I wasn't so sure. I never wear any item of clothing twice in a row, even my Anne Klein jacket, and definitely not a T-shirt I have sweated into. But I didn't want to look like a traitor to my friends. It was just the least of my many worries right then.

Life had become very confusing. I wanted to go to Sandhurst and become a tennis star, but I didn't want to leave my friends. I wanted to stay true to our new cause and keep away from boys, but deep down I still missed Danny. And if I went to Sandhurst, I'd never have to see him again. I didn't know if that was good or bad.

It was the feeling that I had nothing to lose that

made me show up on Tuesday with the T-shirt on again. I brought another top to change into, just in case my friends had chickened out before me, but there they all were, standing out like sore thumbs in their shirts. A couple of girls stopped us before school and said that they agreed with us one hundred percent. Boys did need to be taught a lesson. They suggested that maybe we should hold our meeting after the dance, since most girls were already committed to going to it.

Best of all, the editor of the school newspaper, Susan Schmidt, told us she wanted to do an article on our movement. She said she thought it was really great that freshmen were so politically and socially aware.

"When I was your age, I was just praying that a guy would invite me to the prom—any guy, I didn't care, as long as I wasn't left out," she said with an easy laugh.

Roni and I exchanged glances. I knew just how she felt. Frankly I didn't want to be left out from the dance either. I'd have happily gone with any guy—or almost any guy, nerds excepted. I'm not sure they count as guys, anyway.

I wasn't going to tell my friends about Sandhurst, but you know me—I just can't keep secrets very well. If I have good news, I want the whole world to know it. So my friends got it out of me pretty easily.

"What's with you, Justine?" Karen asked me at

lunchtime on Tuesday. "Did you just ace that English test?"

"The English test? What makes you think I aced the English test?"

"Because you keep bouncing up and down and humming to yourself," Karen said.

"Yeah, Justine. You do look pleased with yourself today," Ginger agreed.

"You haven't made up with Danny, have you?" Roni asked.

"No, I haven't made up with Danny or aced any English test," I said. "Okay, I guess I have to tell you. I wasn't going to, but you'll have to know in the end."

"What? What?"

They crowded around me now. "Is it your secret admirer? Did you find out who he was?"

"No!" I said. "The Boyfriend Club was supposed to be doing that for me. It's nothing like that. I might be transferring to Sandhurst."

They looked really surprised. "Sandhurst? You're going to leave Alta Mesa? Why?"

I felt myself blushing. "They have a great tennis program, and the coach has offered me a scholarship. He needs me on their team right now."

"But isn't it another snobby school like Sagebrush?"

Roni said. "Haven't you always told us how unhappy you were there?"

"I didn't say I was unhappy. It was a great school—it had first-rate facilities, hundreds of tennis courts, a fencing program, ballet . . ."

"But you said you never had any real friends there."

"Not like us," Karen said quietly. "We thought you liked it here, Justine. We thought you were happy, until that stupid fight with Danny."

"I guess I was," I said, swallowing back the lump that was forming in my throat. "But I have to try for success, don't I?"

Karen was looking troubled. "I don't know, Justine. I had a chance to go to a music academy once. But I couldn't think of anything worse than being stuck with music all day every day."

"And being stuck with snobby people all day every day will not be good for you, Justine," Roni said firmly. "You'll be back to your old self, bragging and making stupid remarks that upset everyone."

"No I won't," I said. "I knew you guys would act like this. That's why I didn't want to tell you. If you were my real friends, you'd want what's best for me."

"We do want what's best for you," Karen said. "And we don't think it's Sandhurst."

"Not even if I become a tennis star?"

"Think about it, Justine," Ginger said. "You're a good player, sure. But how many good players are there in Arizona? And then multiply that by fifty states. The chances of turning pro are pretty slim, aren't they?"

Roni was nodding agreement. "It's like Drew is a great wide receiver, but he's not already talking about being drafted by the Cardinals. And he's not letting it run his life either."

"And what if you spent four years at Sandhurst surrounded by horrible snobs, and then you weren't outstanding enough in tennis? You'd have given up your chance to have fun and friends," Karen said.

"They're not all horrible snobs," I said. "The girls I spoke to were very nice and friendly. They can't help having rich parents."

"Remember what happened when you got involved with the Kestrels here?" Ginger pointed out. "They were real friendly to you, to get you to join their sorority, but they weren't nice people. They were completely snobby and rude and into drinking and parties, too. I've heard there's a lot of drugs at those private schools."

"I guess Justine has to make her own decision," Karen said slowly. "It's not right for us to try to stand in her way if she dreams of becoming a tennis star. We should be glad for her that she's been given this chance, even if we will miss her."

"That's right, Justine," Ginger said. "I never thought I'd hear myself say this, but it won't be the same if you go."

"No, Justine," Roni said. "Who will we have to tease about Sagebrush if you leave? Life will be boring."

I felt tears well up in my eyes, and I squeezed them shut to keep from crying. "Shut up, you guys. It's hard enough for me to make this decision without you being nice."

"Speaking of hard decisions," Ginger said. Her gaze drifted down the path to where Ben was standing with a group of friends. I saw him glance in her direction, then pretend that he hadn't seen her. "I'm beginning to wish we hadn't started this no boys thing. I'm feeling bad about it already. Did we overreact, guys?"

"No way," Roni said. "Ben treated you like dirt last weekend."

"I know," Ginger said with a sigh, "but he stopped by to see me last night and tried to apologize. At least, I think that's what he was trying to do. He said he'd go to the dance if it meant so much to me. But you'd have been proud of me. I told him it was okay. I was quite happy to go without him. I don't think he could believe it. Then he got all huffy and said, fine if that was how I wanted it. Then he left and I felt bad."

"We have to be strong, you guys," Roni said. "If we give in now, we won't have achieved anything."

"Except for losing nice boyfriends," Karen said. "James pretended that he didn't care I was going without him, but I know that he does care. He's just too insecure to say so."

"Same with Chris," Roni said.

Ginger gave a big sigh. "Our first real Valentine's Dance and we'll be dancing by ourselves," she said. "Talk about unromantic! I know in my head that these boys have to learn how to respect girls, but my heart wants to give in right now."

"I agree," Karen said. "I can't imagine being at a dance without James, but I have to go through with it. I have to let him see that my feelings count, too."

"Good luck," I said bitterly. "I hoped that Danny would realize that my feelings counted, but he never did. I don't think guys know diddly about feelings. And they only think about themselves. We're better off without them."

"If you say so, Justine," Karen said sadly.

"I guess you're right," Ginger agreed.

I looked at my friends' faces. They were megadepressed. I'd thought at the time that we were being a little hasty when we decided to cut boys out of our lives. Now I was sure of it. I longed for a romantic Valentine's Dance. I felt a little glow inside when I remembered that card with the big red heart from my unknown admirer.

As I looked from one depressed face to the next, it occurred to me that possibly we were wrecking our lives. Ben and James and even Chris-the-Nerd were essentially nice guys, most of the time. Even more important, Ginger and Karen and Roni thought they were special. What if the boys were so upset by this thing that they never came back? Would Ginger really be happier without Ben? Would Karen be happier without James? Okay, so Roni would probably be happier without Chris and back with Drew, but . . .

Wait a minute! I'd just had the world's most brilliant idea! Trust me to think of the perfect solution. I always suspected I was a genius when it came to social activities. I knew a way to make everything right again! It was so simple that I almost laughed out loud.

"What now, Justine?" Karen asked. "You're humming to yourself again."

"Nothing," I said, still smiling. "Nothing at all."

Chapter

13

I could barely get through the rest of the day, I was so excited. As soon as I left school, I went right to the mall. In the Hallmark store I found the biggest and best Valentine's cards and rushed home with them. Then, in my very best penmanship, I began to write:

Dear Ginger,
    You are the most beautiful and special girl in the school. I've been too shy to tell you that myself. Meet me at the Valentine's Dance, by the big

palm tree, outside the back door of the gym, at nine-fifteen.
Love,
Your Secret Admirer.

Then I picked up a plain piece of paper.

Dear Ben,
You could lose your girlfriend if you don't wake up! Another boy is really interested in her. Be outside the back door of the gym Friday at nine-fifteen sharp if you don't want to lose her forever.

I did the same for Karen and James, only I made their rendezvous five minutes later and I gave them a different palm tree. I wanted to be able to spy on both couples. As I sat back to admire my work and start on Roni's, I had a brilliant idea. I wouldn't get Roni back with Chris. I'd get her back with Drew. So I wrote two cards with the secret admirer message. Maybe if they found each other in the darkness outside the gym, at nine-twenty-five precisely, they would realize that they were still in love and everything would be great again.

I couldn't wait for the dance to see my grand scheme in action. Justine, the brilliant matchmaker! I got to school early the next morning, put the cards in the right lockers, and then finished off my plan by ordering three red roses to be delivered to my three friends in class on Friday. That should convince them that their mystery guys meant business!

Satisfied, I went to my locker. When I opened it, another card fell out. In the excitement I'd almost forgotten about my own mystery admirer. I ripped it open. It was a picture of Superman. The text read, "With you at my side I could leap tall buildings and conquer the world. From your secret admirer." Underneath in smaller letters was written, "I am counting the hours until we can finally be together."

I grabbed my friends as soon as they showed up. "Look at this, another card!" I yelled.

They examined it.

"He's counting the hours until you can be together," Ginger sighed. "How romantic. Maybe you've just found yourself the one sweet, romantic guy in the entire school, Justine!"

"You guys were supposed to be finding out who he is," I said.

"Oh, yeah," Roni agreed. "With all the excitement about our anti-boy protest, it must have slipped our minds. We should get onto it."

"But, Justine, are you sure you want to be involved with a guy again?" Karen asked. "Wouldn't that be letting down our cause?"

"If he's as sweet and romantic as the cards he sends, then the answer is yes," I said. "I hope you guys don't mind, but I'd really like to be able to dance the slow dances with a partner. I'd feel stupid with my arms wrapped around myself!"

Roni was examining the card. "This is exciting, Justine. I wonder who it is? Any ideas?"

I shook my head. "And the suspense is killing me," I said. I wasn't ready to tell them my suspicions about Hal yet, just in case I was wrong. "I really do need to find out, you guys. I mean, what if someone taps me on the shoulder at the dance and it turns out to be Owen, or even worse, Walter?"

"I don't think it can be one of the nerds," Roni said. "If they had a crush on you, they'd come right out and say so."

"She's right, Justine," Karen agreed. "This is not nerd-like behavior. This is definitely a shy, sensitive, romantic guy."

167

"And if he doesn't look like a total geek, he'll be perfect," I said. "So come on, you guys. I'm counting on the Boyfriend Club. You have one day to complete your assignment. Find out who my secret admirer is before the dance."

Then I watched as they went to their own lockers and discovered their cards. I heard Ginger say, "What? What is this?"

"What's up?" I asked her.

"Oh—nothing," she said, but her face was red as she stuffed the card into her backpack. Okay, so she wasn't going to admit to anything yet, but I'd definitely gotten her rattled.

The bell rang, so I didn't get a chance to see what Karen and Roni thought about their secret admirers. But I didn't care. On Friday night I'd have them all safely reunited with their special guys. I was the only one who had a big question mark still hanging over her.

As soon as school got out on Thursday, I was waiting on the front steps to grab my friends.

"Okay, tell me, what did you find?"

They looked uneasy. "About what?"

"About my secret admirer, of course. I said this was an assignment for the Boyfriend Club. Don't tell me you didn't do anything about it?"

Now they looked embarrassed and apologetic.

"Sorry, Justine. We didn't find anything," Roni said.

"Nothing at all? What kind of Boyfriend Club is this?" I demanded. "We started the dumb club in the first place so that we didn't have to do our own snooping."

"It's a big school, Justine," Karen said softly. "Three thousand kids. We can't interview them all in a single day."

"Just the guys," I said. "Fifteen hundred guys. How hard can that be? On second thought, make that fourteen hundred and ninety-nine. Danny wouldn't have sent the card."

"Well, we did get started for you." Ginger said. "We made up a list of all the guys who take classes with you or who might have met you through Danny or at football games. What else is there?"

"Someone who has admired me from afar? Someone who saw me in the halls and fell instantly in love with me?"

"Justine, we can hardly go up to every strange guy in the school and say 'Excuse me, but we're doing a survey. Have you secretly fallen in love recently? If so, with whom?'" Roni said, making us all smile, even me.

"You've forgotten about the tennis team," I said. "My secret admirer might be on the team with me."

"Yeah, right," Ginger said. "I thought you told us that they all hated your guts. You said they teased you and were mad at you for having Danny kicked off."

"Maybe one of them is only pretending to hate me,"

I said. "Maybe deep down he's fallen in love with me and can't confess it openly because he'd be teased, too."

"I thought you said the freshman guys were all runts," Ginger commented. "In that case, are you sure you want to meet your secret admirer at the dance? I thought you were the kind of girl who would rather eat liver than dance with a guy who came up to your shoulder."

"There are sophomores on the team too, you know," I said mysteriously. "In fact, there's one sophomore you might want to check out for me. Remember I told you about Hal? Well, he's totally cool and I think . . . I have a sneaking suspicion that he's the one."

"What makes you think that?" Roni asked sharply.

"He admired my drop shot yesterday, and when he said he might be going to the dance, he looked in my direction," I said. "You see, I've discovered more than the Boyfriend Club!"

"He admired your drop shot?" Ginger spluttered. "Is that a hint that a guy likes you?"

Karen frowned at her. "Has he given any other indication that he likes you?" she asked.

"No, but he's shy, remember?" I said. "He's the silent, sensitive type. He probably doesn't want to be teased about liking me." I looked at them excitedly. "I really hope it is him. I can just see Danny's face if I start dating a good-looking sophomore who is also better at

170

tennis than he is! That would just serve him right."

"You sound like you've gotten over Danny already," Karen said.

"Me? Sure I'm over him, that little jerk. I'm only surprised it took me so long to see through him," I said. "Now I'm totally ready to move on to older, more mature guys. No more dating immature little freshmen for me."

"Do you really mean that, Justine?" Roni said, glancing at Karen. "What if Danny's really sorry, but he doesn't know how to make up with you? What if you two got together and he begged you to come back to him? Wouldn't you do it?"

"That's not going to happen," I snapped. "He's sat behind me in class every day and he's pretended that I wasn't there. Face it, guys. He's still really mad. He'll never forgive me, so I'd better just forget about him and get on with my life. Roni, you know sophomores. Do you think you could find out anything about Hal before the dance?"

"I'll try," Roni said, "but if he's as shy as you say, then he'd hardly have confessed his secret love to anyone else. I think you'll just have to wait and see if another card shows up and gives us any more clues."

"I know what I can do," I said excitedly. "I'm going to get to school real early tomorrow morning and hide where I can watch the lockers. That way I can catch my secret admirer delivering the next message. I just hope the whole thing isn't a mean joke."

"Do you think someone would go to the trouble of sending a big, expensive card as a joke?" Ginger asked, looking worried. I could read her like a book. She was wondering if her own secret admirer card was a joke, too.

"No, forget I even said it," I said hastily.

"I'm sure it isn't a joke, Justine," Karen said soothingly. "Even all the tennis guys couldn't hate you that much."

This was probably true. I couldn't see any of those guys going to the trouble of sending me expensive cards when they could easily have tripped me up or pulled some other stunt on the tennis court. Besides, their teasing seemed to have stopped. They had grudgingly admitted that I could play tennis and that I was on the team to stay. So my hunch about Hal had to be right . . . didn't it?

I was up and ready to leave the house just after seven the next morning. Christine appeared in her robe and stopped in surprise when she saw me in the kitchen. "My goodness, what's gotten into you?" she said. "This must be an early rising record. Two mornings in a row. Are you going for the Guinness Book, or is it a before-school meeting?"

"Yes," I said. "A meeting with destiny," and I swept out triumphantly, jogging all the way to school. I stepped into the empty hallway and darted into the girls' bathroom at the far end. If I kept the door half closed, I could get a pretty good view of my locker.

I waited and waited. Girls started coming into the bathroom, giving me funny looks as I let them in, then stayed by the door.

"What's happening?" some of them asked, and I told them that I was trying to catch the person who had vandalized my locker. I watched Roni, Ginger, and Karen arrive. I watched the halls fill with students. I stayed at my post until the first bell rang, but then I was forced to come out and get my books for first period. As I opened my locker, another envelope fell out. I was so surprised that I jumped. I was beginning to think that I had a phantom admirer!

"How did he manage it?" I exclaimed. "I was watching my locker since seven-thirty. Nobody went near it!"

Roni saw me and came running over. "Another card? Let's see!"

Ginger and Karen followed her. As I took it out they all went "Ooohhh" in unison.

This one was really special. The heart was red satin. The message read "My heart belongs to you," and the small, neat printing said, "Meet me at the Valentine's Dance tonight. Only a few more hours until we're together, my love."

"He wants me to meet him at the dance," I yelled, then blushed when half the school seemed to turn around and grin.

"That's great, Justine," Karen said.

"I hope it's great," I said. "I still don't know if it's the boy of my dreams or my nightmares. I wonder if he'll just come up and introduce himself at the dance. Or do you think he'll send me another message and arrange a time and place to meet? Ooh, this is so romantic, guys. Nothing like this has ever happened to me before."

"I don't think this is true to the principles of our No Boys movement," Ginger said, "but in this case, we forgive you and we understand."

"Yeah, we can understand that secret admirers are something really special," Karen said, blushing.

"Maybe not all boys are jerks," Roni said.

"Maybe we should change our slogan to No More Jerks," Karen cracked.

I grinned to myself all the way through first period. I had never felt so special before. Some boy liked me enough to send me all these beautiful cards. Some boy was longing to get together with me at the right place and time. He had to be a romantic, didn't he? Most guys wouldn't think of doing something sweet like that. They'd just stop me in the halls and yell, "Yo, Justine. Wanna come to the dance with me?"

I refused to believe that my admirer was a runt or a nerd or in any other way disgusting. He'd be quiet and serious and perfect in every way. And Danny would drop dead with jealousy!

The school day went on. Then, during sixth period, the classroom door opened, and a student council member came in. "Valentine deliveries for the following students," he announced. "Karen Nguyen, Ginger Hansen, Angie Wester, Roni Ruiz, Sondra White, Justine Craft."

Roni and Ginger exchanged very surprised looks, and I heard them whispering to each other as their flowers were delivered. I saw Karen's face go as red as the rose as she took the flower. It went even brighter red when she saw the message I'd sent with it: "From your secret admirer. I can't wait to meet you in person." I only wished that Ben and Drew and James had been in the classroom to see it. But I didn't have any more time to think of that, because the messenger was heading for me with a red rose in his hand.

I took my red rose with trembling hands. I could hardly wait to open the card. It said, "The band will play our song at nine-thirty. I'll be waiting outside the back entrance to the gym to meet you."

Nine-thirty—the timing was perfect. I'd have time to spy on my friends and then move on to my own date with destiny! And our song! The guy was perfect. I kept on staring at those neatly printed words on the card. He had nice writing, too. That was good. I hated sloppy guys. I bet he dressed well.

At tennis practice I kept looking for signs that Hal was the one. I was dying to bring up the subject of red roses or Valentine's cards, but we had a doubles tournament coming up on Saturday morning—The Heart Association Valentine's Day Invitational, called very sweetly the Valentine's Love Match—and Don worked us so hard that we had no time or energy for chitchat. Hal left as soon as practice was over.

He's just shy, I told myself. *Tonight at the dance, he'll become the love of my life.*

Chapter

14

As soon as I got home from practice, I began experimenting with my hair. I wanted to look not too old but not too young, not too sexy but not too innocent. In the end I put it up with a red silk rose in it. This seemed the right thing to do, since he'd sent me a red rose. And it went perfectly with the red dress I'd finally bought at the mall.

Next I spent half an hour doing my nails. By seven-thirty there was nothing else I could possibly have done to improve the way I looked. I imagined how his eyes would light up when he saw me. "Justine, you look perfect," he'd whisper. "You look like a dream come true." And then the band would play our song and he'd take me in his arms and we'd slow dance . . . I wasn't totally sure what our song would be, or how he'd get the band to play it at the right time, but I figured that if the band was playing a really gross rap song at nine-thirty, I'd stay inside the gym!

My dad drove me to school around eight o'clock. I'd been too nervous to eat anything, and now my stomach was giving annoying rumbles. I'd have to stuff in a few chips as soon as I got to the dance. I couldn't meet the new love of my life with a rumbly tummy.

Dark shapes were already streaming into the gym as I got out of my dad's car. The music was already playing so loudly that I could feel the beat through the soles of my feet.

I went to the pillar by the front entrance where Karen, Roni, and Ginger were waiting for me. It was clear they'd all taken a whole lot of trouble with their appearance.

"Justine, you look great," Karen called out as she saw me. "I bet your secret admirer's eyes will bulge right out of his head when he sees you."

"You guys look good too," I said. "Sexy dress, Ginger."

Ginger frowned. "Just because we're at a dance alone doesn't mean we have to look boring," she said hastily.

"And you never know who you might meet at a dance," I said with a big smile.

The music was super loud, and the gym was unrecognizable: dark except for the pink spotlight sparkling on the revolving globe, the whole ceiling hung with red and pink balloons, and a rainbow of heart-shaped balloons over the stage where the band was playing. It looked very pretty—amazingly pretty when you consider that it was a public high school gym.

I looked around at the sea of faces, wondering which was the one. Was he standing in sight of the door, watching me come in now? It was too dark to see. We got a table and chairs in a corner and then we went to get punch and popcorn. Then we danced, by ourselves, then sat and talked, then danced again. And all the time I didn't stop looking. I was sure my admirer must be watching me, maybe walking past my table a few times to make sure I was there. Maybe he was now dancing right beside me on the floor and I didn't even know it.

I noticed that my friends were looking, too. We were all very tense. I just prayed that Ben and James were here. I could see Drew, dancing with his wild friends. Drew was always everywhere. Such a fun guy, so right for Roni.

By about nine o'clock I found that I could hardly breathe. The minutes seemed like hours. My friends were equally jumpy, all pretending to dance, but none of us paying any attention to the music. Karen even went on shaking her arms up and down for about a minute after the song had ended.

"Phew, it's hot in here," Ginger said. "Excuse me, guys, but I have to go outside to get some air."

I grinned to myself as she left. Plan one on schedule. A little while later Karen decided that she needed to get more punch and she disappeared.

"I might as well go to the rest room, while the others have vanished," Roni said casually, and she strolled toward the back door.

That left just me. I knew what I had to do. I sprinted around to the front entrance, so that I could sneak up on each of the encounters from behind. By this time I really did need some air. I was finding it so hard to breathe that I felt I was going to faint any moment. I went out of the front door and stood gulping in the cool night air, trying to stop my knees from shaking.

Then I saw him. Hal had come out of the dance and was standing in the darkness a few feet away from me. He was early, but this had to be the sign. He must have followed me to the door. I couldn't stand the tension a moment longer.

"Hi, Hal," I said softly into the darkness.

He jumped. "Oh—uh, hi, Justine. I didn't see you standing there."

"It was hot in there. I had to get some fresh air," I said.

"Yeah, it was hot," he agreed.

There was a long pause.

"Were you . . . looking for someone?"

"Um, sort of."

He sort of smiled, that faraway, mysterious smile, as he nodded and looked at me for the first time.

"You don't have to wait until nine-thirty, you know," I heard myself blurting out. "It was a really sweet idea . . . all the cards were sweet. . . ."

He was looking at me strangely now, as if I'd turned into a new and dangerous animal. "What are you talking about?"

Luckily I didn't have to answer this. I saw Hal's face light up. "Hey, Brenda, over here," he called.

A girl in a frilly dress came teetering up on very spiked heels. "Have you been waiting long?" she cooed. "Sorry I couldn't get here earlier. I only just got off work."

Then she slipped her arm through his, and they went into the dance together, leaving me standing, hot with embarrassment, in the cool night air. How could I have been so stupid? How could I have got it so wrong? I squirmed as I realized how close I had come to making a total fool of myself. And now there was another question. If Hal wasn't my secret admirer, who was?

I stood there, taking deep breaths, trying to calm down. I'd just almost made one big boo-boo. I couldn't afford to screw up anything else. It was nine-fifteen. Time for Ginger's rendezvous with Ben. I put my racing thoughts in order and tiptoed around the corner. I saw them standing there, by the big palm tree. I couldn't hear what they were saying, but I heard raised voices. This wasn't going too well. Then I heard Ginger say, "Oh, I get it now. It was you all the time!"

And suddenly she fell into Ben's arms. They were now in the middle of a long, tender kiss and they didn't see me as I tiptoed by to find Karen and James. I was just a little too late for them. They were already standing with their arms around each other, and he was saying, "How could I ever have doubted you?"

Karen replied, "We were so dumb to fight about nothing."

Then they kissed. This was becoming monotonous.

Roni and Drew weren't even at the spot I'd selected for them. Either they'd already met or they'd chickened out. I just hoped that they'd found each other and made up instantly.

Inside the dance the band had started playing Whitney Houston's "I Will Always Love You," which just happens to be one of my very favorite songs. Chills started going up and down my spine. I looked at my watch. Almost nine-thirty. My heart started pounding again. I didn't want to go around to the back door of the gym, but I knew I had to. Destiny was waiting for me.

A figure was standing in the shadows of the back entrance. He was tall, but not too tall, slim but not skinny, dressed in a dark suit. I heaved a sigh of relief. At least it wasn't Owen. I took a deep breath and then stepped into the shadows as the lead singer belted out, "And I . . . will always love you. . . ."

"Hi," I said softly.

The figure wheeled around at the sound of my voice. He had expected me to be coming from the dance floor. "Hi," he said in a low, sexy voice that was somehow familiar. "I'm glad you came."

We moved together into the light of the outside security lamp and got a good look at each other for the first time.

"You?" he exclaimed in a horrified voice.

"You?" I heard myself echo.

It was Danny. For a second my heart soared—Danny was my secret admirer! He hadn't wanted to admit that he was wrong in public. That's why he'd arranged this secret meeting. He was lost without me. He wanted us to get back together again. It was sweet. It was wonderful. It was a miracle.

"Danny, what are you doing here?" I began, taking a step toward him. But the look in his eyes made me stop.

"What are *you* doing here?" he asked rudely.

183

"I'm supposed to be meeting someone."

"So am I."

A big grin spread across his face. "Oh, I get it, Justine. So you couldn't live without me after all. I should have known. Boy, is this sweet! Who would have thought that the famous tennis star, Justine Craft, couldn't stand to be without me."

He was laughing at me. Either this was just a horrible coincidence that we were outside the gym at the same moment, each waiting for someone else, or it was a mean trick he'd played to get even.

"What makes you think I came out here to meet you?" I demanded. My nerves were now stretched to the breaking point, and I was annoyed that he'd seen my hopeful expression when I recognized him.

He was still grinning easily, still looking as if he'd just scored a point. "You mean you didn't send me the note that told me to meet you out here? Strange that you just happened to be at this very spot at the same time as me . . . or did you find out about the hot babe I was supposed to get together with and come to spy on us?"

"Excuse me?" I snapped. "I came to meet my secret admirer. He sent me notes and flowers all week, which is more than you've ever done."

"*Your* secret admirer? I got cards from *my* secret admirer. She said she had the biggest crush on me."

"Then she must need glasses," I said angrily.

"And your secret admirer must be really weird, or he wouldn't want to date a girl who has to prove herself by going out for guys' teams. I hope he doesn't mind getting his ego stepped on all the time."

"His ego can't be as big as yours. It's only guys like you, with an ego the size of Texas, who have problems."

"I do not have a big ego."

"Let's put it this way," I said angrily. "I hear they're having to alter all the doors at this school, just to let your head through."

"Oh, I thought that was so that you didn't hit anyone when you swung your tennis racket."

"I'm not the person who got kicked off the team."

Danny looked around impatiently. "I'm wasting my time here. It's pretty clear the girl isn't going to come while you're hanging around. So congratulations, Justine. You just screwed up something else in my life."

"Did it occur to you that you screwed up my life too? I was supposed to meet a guy here at nine-thirty. Obviously he's a shy, sensitive type, and he backed away when he saw you. He said the band would be playing our song."

Now he was looking at me strangely again. "That's what my note said."

"That's really weird."

"Are you sure you didn't send me the note to trick me into meeting you?" he asked.

"In your dreams. I was hoping to get together with a more mature guy and forget all about you."

"Hah, so you haven't forgotten about me!"

"Only because you keep on showing up when I don't want you to."

"So how do you explain this, huh?" he demanded. "I get notes, you get notes, and they both say the same thing. . . ."

"It sounds like some stupid person is trying to get us back together again," I began. Then I stopped, horrified. What had I just been trying to pull off with my friends? I'd been trying to get them back together again with their boyfriends—which was exactly what they'd been trying to do to me.

This finally began to make sense. I remembered that Roni and Ginger and Karen had been close to my locker while I'd been keeping watch. Any one of them could have slipped the card inside, and I'd never have caught on. It was just the sort of thing they would do.

"My friends," I moaned. "I bet it's my dumb friends."

"Then you can tell them they're wasting their time," Danny said coldly. "You made me look like a fool, Justine. Why would anyone think we'd want to get back

186

together again?" He pushed past me and disappeared into the night.

I stood there in the cool darkness, all alone, listening to the rich throb of music coming from inside. "And I . . . will always love you . . ." It hurt almost more than I could bear. There was no sign of Ginger, Roni, or Karen anywhere. I was very tempted to go straight home and forget the whole, horrible evening. I felt like the world's biggest idiot. Seeing Danny there in the darkness had made me realize that I hadn't gotten over him at all. And now I really had lost him forever, thanks to my stupid, interfering friends. I wasn't going home until I told them what I thought about them.

I pushed past the crowd at the doorway. The first thing I saw as I went back into the gym was Ginger, slow dancing with Ben. Next to her was Karen, dancing with her head on James's shoulder. *Terrific*, I thought. How come my plan works so well and theirs is a hopeless failure? I looked around for Roni. I saw her talking and laughing with Drew. So even that hunch had worked. But wait. Something strange was happening. While Roni and Drew were talking, Chris appeared. What was that nerd doing cutting in on them? He was taking Roni's hand. She was going to dance with him, leaving Drew standing there.

I couldn't stand it a moment longer. I pushed past the dancing couples to Roni and Chris.

"Wait, what are you doing?" I yelled.

"We're dancing. Why?"

"Can I see you a minute?" I said. "I need to talk to Roni for just one second," I said to Chris, and I dragged her away.

"You were supposed to get back together with Drew!" I shouted.

Roni grinned. "So we were right. Drew and I decided that it was either a joke, or one of our friends had to be playing at a little matchmaking. We knew it as soon as we both stepped out of that door at the same time. Nice try, Justine. Thanks but no thanks."

"But you said it yourself," I hissed. "You wanted to go to the dance with Drew."

"I sort of fantasized about it," she said. "After all, he is the cutest guy in the universe. But I decided that I wasn't ready to go through all that again. And I had second thoughts about Chris, too."

"Chris? How could you choose a nerd over a jock?"

She had this sweet, faraway look on her face. "He sent me the sweetest Valentine's card today. And it made me think—was it fair of me to tell him he had to choose between the nerds and me? I mean, how would I feel if a guy told me I had to give up my friends?"

"Your friends are not totally creepy, slimy, and disgusting," I pointed out.

"All the same, I don't have the right to choose his friends for him," she said. "In the card he promised there would be no more nerds. He said I was more important to him than anything else, and if it made me uncomfortable when he hung out with the nerds, then he'd stop. And then I felt bad. I didn't want to have that kind of power over anyone."

"I think you need your head examined," I said.

She looked around. "So what happened with your secret admirer, Justine? Did you meet anyone?" I noticed that Ginger and Karen had left their partners and were closing in on us.

"Yes," I said. "I had a meeting with a jerk, set up by my airheaded friends. Well, thanks a lot. You made me look like a total fool. You got my hopes up for nothing."

"We only wanted to help, Justine," Roni said. "You and Danny seemed so right for each other. And you seemed so miserable without him. We just wanted to get you back together in romantic surroundings."

"Yeah, Justine," Ginger added. "We thought that if you had a chance to talk to each other away from tennis, when you were both looking your best, that you'd realize how much you'd missed each other."

"For your information, Danny would rather have

bumped into King Kong than me. He was hoping to meet another girl, and he was furious when he found out that his dream babe was only me."

"Sorry," Karen said. "We really meant well, Justine. We knew that sometimes it only takes a little push to get people back together again—look at me and James. Whoever planned that little trick was so right. He couldn't stand the thought of losing me. He promised he'd make me feel more special from now on."

"And Ben came home early from his baseball game, to make it to the dance," Ginger said. "He said he'd been miserable all week without me. He didn't admit it, but I bet he was the one who sent me the red rose."

"I didn't think of that," Karen said. "I bet James planned this whole thing to get us back together again. What a sweetie."

Great, so I wasn't even going to get the credit for my expert matchmaking. I could have told them it was me, but why spoil their happiness? If they thought they had sweet, thoughtful guys, then lucky for them. A big sob was building in my throat. Why couldn't Danny have said that he was lost without me? Why was I the only one who ended up with nobody?

"I guess there never was any hope for Danny and me," I said. "We're just too different. I think I'll call my dad to come get me now." I pushed past them and headed for the door. I heard them call after me, but I didn't turn around.

Chapter

15

I couldn't get over what a jerk I had been. I should have known that Danny and I were doomed to failure. We were such opposites in every way—me sophisticated, charming, rich, elegant . . . and he more the redneck type. I was caviar, and he was hot dogs. I was silk, and he was flannel. I was Monte Carlo, and he was Coney Island. Anyway, it was doomed.

And I was better off without him. Now that I knew, one hundred percent, that we'd never get back together, I could think about getting on with my life, finding a new guy, and becoming the best tennis player in the world. Okay, maybe just the best tennis player in Arizona. But at least it had made my decision for me. I now knew that I wanted to get out of Alta Mesa as quickly as possible and transfer to Sandhurst.

I got up the next morning more determined than I had ever been. I was going to play the tournament of my life at this stupid Valentine's thing, and afterward I was going to announce to my surprised and distressed team that I was about to leave them and switch to Sandhurst. Then I'd start a new life, new school, new tennis buddies, new friends. Better friends than those three interfering traitors who had screwed up my life last night.

I wished I had time to swing by the pro shop at my father's country club and pick up a new tennis outfit. But we had to be at the courts at eight-thirty, and nowhere that sells upscale clothing is open at that time. I'd just have to make do with that tacky Alta Mesa T-shirt one more time.

I was so tense, I couldn't even swallow my orange juice. Maybe I was coming down with some terminal disease. Then everyone would be sorry! I could just see them at my funeral—me lying in an open coffin in a suitably angelic white dress, my hair curled adorably over my shoulders. Roni and Ginger would clutch each other in grief, Karen wouldn't be able to muffle her sobs. If only we hadn't played that mean trick on her, she might still be here today, they'd say. And Danny would file past, looking uncomfortable in a dark suit and tie, his hair parted and combed. "Oh, Justine," he'd whisper. "Why did I wait until it was too late to tell you what I really felt about you? How could I have been such a fool? How can I go on living without you?"

The only downside to that was that I wouldn't be around to enjoy it!

By the time I got to the tennis courts, I'd already decided that I'd rather make Danny sick by seeing me as a tennis superstar than by coming to my funeral. Why should I miss out? I tossed back my ponytail and strode up to my team. I pretended I didn't even see Danny standing behind the coach.

Don looked up and gave me a big smile. "Great, here's Justine, now we can get going," he said, as if the whole team had been waiting for me.

"Listen up, team," Don said. "This tournament is all doubles, no singles. On court number four we start with Danny and Justine."

"Excuse me?" both Danny and I said at the same moment.

"You heard me," Don said, looking up with a slight frown. "Danny and Justine, court four. You're playing Washington. Get over there."

"But, Coach," Danny began, "couldn't you put her with Hal and let me play with someone else?"

"You want to be kicked off this team for good,

Pandini?" the coach shouted. "Get over there and start playing."

Danny snatched up his racket and strode out for the court ahead of me. "This is a dumb idea," he snapped.

"Tell me about it," I retorted. "I'm not exactly thrilled about being stuck with a weaker player."

Don came up behind us and put a big hand on each of our shoulders. "Now listen to me," he said. "I don't care what you two feel or don't feel about each other. Right now you're a team and you're representing your high school. I expect you to play hard and play to win, is that clear? Because if not, I can run this program fine without either of you."

"Yes, Coach," we mumbled.

Danny didn't look at me. I didn't look at him. This was like my worst nightmare come true. How could I play on a tennis court beside him? How could I concentrate on my game, knowing he was right there, within touching distance? Maybe that scratchy throat was getting worse? If it was only bad enough, if only I could get a temperature to go with it, then I could drop out and go home.

"I hope I can play," I muttered to Danny. "I'm not feeling so good."

"Don't worry about it," he said. "Nobody expects much from a girl."

Well! I'd show him who was the stronger player in our team. If they weren't expecting much from me, then they were in for a surprise.

As we walked onto the court, two surprised faces were staring at us. "You're the team from Alta Mesa?" one of the Washington players asked. They looked at each other and grinned. "How come you've got a girl playing on your team?" the bigger one said. "Are all the guys at your school total wimps?"

"You wait until you see her play," Danny said aggressively. "Then you'll know why."

I looked at him in surprise. Danny had actually said something nice about me? I took out my racket and started warming up. The Washington guys were still grinning. I could tell they thought this first-round match was a gimme for them. The first ball they sent across the net was definitely intended to scare me. But I just whacked it right back. They weren't smiling quite so much now.

We started to play. They were good, and they were consistent. Everything we sent at them they returned. They had us running all over the court. I was concentrating so hard I actually forgot that my partner was Danny. We fought for every point. We won some and lost some. The games were pretty even. Then I rushed the net and the guy opposite me hit the ball as hard as he could right at me. This time I couldn't move fast enough. It hit me square in the middle. I tried to breathe, but no breath would come. I sat down hard on the court, and everything spun around. My insides felt like they were on fire.

"Hey, that was a cheap shot!" Danny yelled.

"It's a shot I'd have made to any guy," my opponent shouted back. "If she can't hack it with the guys, then she should get back where she belongs."

"She can hack it just fine, and you know it," Danny shouted back, although he'd said exactly the same thing himself not too long ago. "Only weak players who can't win fair and square have to start hitting their opponents."

He knelt down beside me. "Are you okay?" he asked.

I nodded, pointing to my middle. "I just can't breathe," I managed to hiss.

"Oh, don't tell me she's going to cry now," one of the guys said, nudging his partner as they stood looking down at me.

"Hey, we're in the middle of a game here," the tall Washington guy yelled. "No time out allowed. Either get on with it or forfeit."

Danny's hand was on my shoulder. "We don't have to go on playing if you don't want to," he said softly. "We don't have to take this from a couple of jerks. Let them have their win if it makes them happy. Who cares?"

I fought to get air inside me and struggled to my feet. "It's okay," I said, rubbing my middle, which felt as if there was a big hole in it. "I'm okay. I say we play on and beat the pants off those guys."

He looked at me in delight. "Let's do it," he muttered.

After that we played as if we were possessed. We dove for impossible shots, we reached impossible overheads, we returned impossible serves. I had no idea Danny could play so well when he tried. To tell you the truth, I had no idea I could either. We were beating the stuffing out of them when one of them sent a shot right down the center line.

"Yours," Danny and I both yelled at the same moment.

The ball went right between us.

For a second we just stood there, glaring at each other. Then Danny's lips started to twitch. I started to grin, too, and suddenly we both burst out laughing.

"Justine, I've missed you," Danny said.

"I've missed you too, you dope," I said.

And we just fell into each other's arms in the middle of the tennis court.

"I've been a real jerk, Jus," Danny said, his eyes looking down warmly into mine. "I don't know what made me act so dumb. I just didn't know how to handle competing with you. Then I didn't know how to make up again without looking like a wimp. I've been so mad at myself. . . . Forgive me?"

"Of course I forgive you," I said.

"Come on, ref. This is a tennis game. They can't hold us up like this! Make them get on with it or forfeit," the Washington player screamed.

Danny looked at me and winked. "Let's continue this later, okay?"

"Okay," I said.

Fifteen minutes later we had beaten them, six-three. Outside the fence there was wild screaming. "Yeah, Justine! Way to go!"

I looked up and there were Roni, Karen, and Ginger, leaping up and down like crazy. I ran over to them. "What are you guys doing here?"

"We thought you might need a cheering section," Roni said, "but you look like you're doing fine without us."

"We're sorry about last night," Karen said. "We all felt that you and Danny really wanted to get back together but didn't know how."

"And your matchmaking worked," Ginger said with a knowing smile. "I just wish ours had. We were so sure!"

"You were right," I said. "It took a tennis match to do it."

My friends broke into smiles. "Really?" Karen asked. "You and Danny are back together?"

I nodded happily.

"So you forgive us?" Ginger said. "You'll come sleep over at Roni's tonight?"

"And come watch our track meet tomorrow? Guess what? James is coming to cheer. So is Chris."

"So is Ben," Ginger said. "I couldn't believe it."

"It looks like we won our campaign after all," I said, looking across at Danny waiting for me by the gate.

"I'd better go," I said. "We have another match to play. See you guys later."

I ran to catch up with Danny. But before I could reach him, a beautiful blond girl stepped up and tapped me on the shoulder. "Nice playing, Justine," she said. "You're just what we need at Sandhurst. And I bet you're dying to join us, aren't you?" Before I could answer, she glanced across at my friends in the stands. "That's the trouble with public schools," she whispered. "Too many minorities, right?"

She was talking about my friends! What a snob! Now I remembered all the things I had chosen to forget about private school: the catty whispers, the put-downs, always acting superior and looking down on anyone who was different. That was how Sagebrush had been, and that's how Sandhurst would be as well. I hadn't realized how much I had changed!

I faced the Sandhurst girl with a sweet smile. "You're right," I said. "We have a lot of minorities at public school. And luckily snobs are a minority at mine."

Then I pushed past her. I'd tell her coach thanks but no thanks. Danny and I would make a great team at Alta Mesa. He held out his hand to me as I ran to catch up with him.

"What was that all about?" he asked.

"Nothing," I said. "Nothing important. Just some dumb private-school thing." I smiled at him.

He was looking at me in a way that made me want to melt. "I can't believe this, Jus," he said. "I thought I'd lost you."

"I thought you hated my guts."

"The only person I was angry at was me," he said. "I know I lost it that first time you showed up on the tennis court, and I felt so bad afterward. But then I didn't know what to do to make things right. Every time I started to say something to you, it all got twisted around until we said horrible things to each other."

"You said horrible things to me at the dance," I reminded him.

"I know. Only because I was hurt. I thought you were excited about meeting someone else. I thought you'd gotten over me."

I looked at him tenderly. "I never got over you. I was hurting all the time."

"It's so hard, isn't it?"

"What is?"

"Boys and girls. Why can't we just come out and say what we feel?"

"We should, if we really trust each other."

He took my hands and pulled me close to him. "You can trust me, Justine. I promise I'll never act like that again." He bent his face toward mine and kissed me gently. We just stood there, right beside the tennis courts as the crowd watched us. At least, I think they were watching us. I didn't really notice. All that mattered was me and Danny and his lips warm against mine.

"Hey, Craft, Pandini. Get over here right now. You're due on court three," Don's voice broke us hastily apart.

Danny gave me a sort of embarrassed grin. "We better get over there," he said. "You ready to kick some more butt?"

"You better believe it."

"Let's go, then." He was holding my hand and he started to run. We were flying together with no effort at all. We were a team. We were invincible.

About the Author

Janet Quin-Harkin has written over fifty books for teenagers, including the best-seller *Ten-Boy Summer*. She is the author of the *Friends* series, the *Heartbreak Café* series, and the *Senior Year* series. She has also written several romances.

Ms. Quin-Harkin lives with her husband in San Rafael, California. She has four children. In addition to writing books, she teaches creative writing at a nearby college.

**THE BEST OF
THE
ADVICE
EXCHANGE**

Boyfriend Club Central asked:

What should you do when you want to date but your parents say you're not old enough?

We got so many good responses that we're printing more of your advice:

Don't get angry. Calm down and think about it. You may be too young after all.

- Kara C., Winston-Salem, NC

Tell the boy you can't date and just be friends.

- Natasha B., Decatur, GA

Stop and think. Maybe you're not old enough. If you think you are, talk to your mom or dad about dating. They will probably say it is difficult to date.
- Heather H., Norwalk, OH

Prove to your parents that you are responsible, mature, and have good judgement. Also, have an open, honest talk with your parents.
- Megan K., Spring, TX

Invite him over to meet your parents so they can get to know him and trust that you are old enough to start dating.
- Kimberly Y., Waldorf, MD

You will have to deal with it. You'll be dating before you know it. Don't try to act older than you are.
- Brandy C., Tekonsha, MI

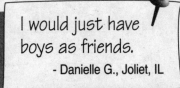
I would just have boys as friends.
- Danielle G., Joliet, IL

The Boyfriend Club ™

You don't need
—— a boyfriend to join! ——

Now you and your friends can join the real Boyfriend Club and receive a special Boyfriend Club kit filled with lots of great stuff only available to Boyfriend Club members.

- **A mini phone book for your special friends' phone numbers**
- **A cool Boyfriend Club pen**
- **A really neat pocket-sized mirror and carrying case**
- **A terrific change purse/keychain**
- **A super doorknob hanger for your bedroom door**
- **The exclusive Boyfriend Club Newsletter**
- **A special Boyfriend Club ID card**

All this for just $3.50!

If you join today, you'll receive your special package and be an official member in 4-6 weeks. Just fill in the coupon below and mail to: The Boyfriend Club, Dept. B, Troll Associates, 100 Corporate Drive, Mahwah, NJ 07430

- -

❏ **Yes,** I want to be a member of the real Boyfriend Club. I have enclosed a check or money order for $3.50 payable to The Boyfriend Club.

Name_____

Address_____

City_____State_____Zip_____

Age_____Where did you buy this book?_____

Sorry, this offer is only available in the U.S.